We Are All Prodigals

By A. M. Nelson

This is a work of fiction. Names, characters, organizations, places and events are the product of the author's imagination or are used fictitiously.

Text copyright © 2015 Angela M. Nelson

Cover Art: Rebekah Croom
rjbusboom.squarespace.com

Dedication:

This book is dedicated to my grandmothers. And to all women who suffer through.

Part One: Flora

CHAPTER ONE

The old greyhound bus rumbled to a stop at the deserted small town station. The doors screeched open, and the elderly driver watched in his mirror as I walked down the narrow aisle. As I went down the steps, he said "Hey," and I turned around.

"Don't you got any luggage, Miss?" he asked.

"No, I don't got any luggage," I said.

"You got someone here to meet you?"

"No, I don't got anyone here to meet me," I answered.

"You got a coat then?"

"No." I folded my arms across my skinny chest and looked away. The night was cold, and all I had on was the thin cotton dress I'd worn on the day I ran away, and the cheap canvas shoes you could buy at the Woolworth's.

For some reason the driver kept on. "You got any money, or

any place to stay?"

"No." My voice quavered. Supposedly there was a town up over the hill, but I didn't see too many lights.

The driver was silent for a long moment, just looking at me with his hand resting on the lever to pull the door closed. I'd seen him looking back at me now and then in his mirror ever since his shift began in Missoula. Because he was older and he was white I stood there patiently, trying not to shiver, looking down at my shoes and wishing he would swing the door shut and let me be. At last he pulled a worn leather wallet out of his pocket, opened it up, and took out a twenty dollar bill. "Here then," he said, looking embarrassed. "Take care of yourself for tonight at least."

I looked up at him, shocked and confused. The idea of taking the man's money was repugnant to me, and my first instinct was to turn on my heel and march away. But I was in no place to refuse any help, and the practical side of me soon won over. I reached out for the bill, stammering, "Thank you, Sir," then looked down at the ground.

"Now, don't you be ashamed of takin' it, Dearie," the driver said firmly, and I looked up. "Most of us could use a bit of help at one time or another, so don't you be ashamed. You look out for yourself now, you hear?"

"All right, I will," I said. Even though he was a white man, his eyes were kind. And I felt the first warm ray of hope since the beginning of my trip spread through me, like melted butter on top of a biscuit. "I will," I said again, and smiled up at him.

The driver gave me a nod, pulled the doors shut, and drove away, leaving me to face the cold night alone. But not quite alone. I had a crisp twenty dollar bill tucked in my dress pocket, and I reached in to touch it. I'd sure never had one of those before. The thick paper felt reassuring against my fingers. I hugged my arms tight around myself, shivering as I walked up a hill and into the town. But on the inside, that warm butter feeling pooled deep inside my chest, and it stayed.

It was October 21st, 1969, and I'd just gotten off the bus in Spring, Idaho, a tiny logging town in the middle of the state's narrow northern strip. I'd never heard of Spring, but it had sounded far away and kind, and I'd needed a new place to start—the farther away the better. When I had spread Momma's money out on the tray at the big city station and asked how far I could go, the lady in the booth had flipped back and forth through the pages of a huge book and said that if I wanted, I could go all the way to Spring. So Spring it was.

The bus had let me out on Front Street, less than a mile off the highway that ran, curve following curve, along a big river. I walked up the street until I hit Main, which veered up past a park and on in to the tiny town. Main Street was narrow and tidy, with glass fronted shops lined up in neat rows on either side. I passed a hardware store, a restaurant, a movie theater, and a donut shop. On either side, steep, black hills seemed to come down right into the town. The streets were empty and quiet. It was about 9:45 p.m. on a

Tuesday night, a time when decent folks were at home getting ready for bed.

I needed a warm place to sleep. There had been a big hotel with a neon flashing sign back by the highway. Twenty dollars was a lot of money, but I figured I'd better make it last and save it for food. A bit farther down Main Street I saw a church—a neat, white, rectangular type of church with a steeple, and I decided I'd try there. There would be long pews to stretch out on, and I would be out of the air at least. Of all the different places I could go, I thought, maybe a church was best. At least there, folks are supposed to help someone like me.

I walked up the painted black steps and pulled open one of the heavy double doors. Inside it was quiet and still. Moonlight shone through a circular stained glass window high up on the wall on the opposite side of the room, highlighting a picture of a yellow cross with red roses and green leaves twining all around. I picked a pew at the front of the church near the window and stretched my long body out on the wooden seat. I fell asleep looking up at that window with the beautiful red roses, with one hand resting on the small firm lump in my middle where a baby now grew, hidden and unseen, beating its little life inside mine. Just before I dropped off to sleep I prayed: Jesus, please take care of my baby. I need a safe, warm home for my baby. I just kept begging God please.

CHAPTER TWO

When I woke up the morning sun was streaming down in red, yellow, and green stripes on my dress. At first I couldn't remember where I was. Then I looked up and saw the window with the roses. My body hurt from sleeping on the hard wood bench. As I came to, I soon realized I wasn't alone, because I heard the sound of a man clearing his throat across the room.

I sat right up, patting my hair and smoothing my dress over my knees, startled and alert as a cat. Then I looked cautiously around at the man across the room. Must be the janitor, I thought, since he wore an apron and carried a dustpan and broom. When I looked at him he looked away. He was white, not very big or tall, and had gray hair that stuck up a little in the back from a cowlick. "Excuse me, Miss," he said. "I didn't want to disturb you, but I thought I'd better wake you up somehow, before you woke up on your own and got scared out of your skin."

The man shuffled his feet awkwardly and looked around the

room, looked anywhere but at me. But I was used to that. Most white people did.

"I'm . . . I'm sorry I trespassed, Sir," I said. I tried to keep my voice steady and polite, even though my heart was racing and thumping, and sounded to me as loud as a drum. Then I asked, "Would you please tell me the time?"

"It's eight-fifteen now. Folks might start arriving soon for the Missions Committee meeting soon. Someone will be coming around about eight thirty to start the coffee."

"Oh," I said. "Well, I have to be going anyway. Do you know of any place in town where somebody might want to hire a young lady like me?"

The janitor stopped his sweeping and looked up, meeting my eye. "Well now, I don't rightly know," he answered. "I suppose you could try the shops along Main Street. I heard the drug store was wanting somebody, but they were looking for a boy. I can't say as I can be much help to you there."

"Thank you anyway," I said. "I'm sure something will come up." I turned to walk down the aisle to the double doors and go, but he called out after me.

"Miss . . . . Will you be needing a place to sleep again tonight?"

I paused and, without turning around, said in as casual voice as I could, "I suppose I might be needing a place."

"The deacons meet here on Wednesdays. They finish up around nine-thirty. So you might wait till ten o'clock or so comes around, when they'll all be gone home."

I turned to give him my most gracious smile. "Thank you Sir. I'll do that."

"You're welcome," he said, and then started in to work again.

I left, closing the door carefully behind me. As I went down the front steps, I thought about how two people had been kind to me in two days. Two white men. Never in my wildest imagination would I have expected that to happen. I reached into my pocket again to finger my twenty dollar bill. And I thought, things just might work out in this place.

CHAPTER THREE

I walked back through town to the public park which I'd seen the night before, hoping to find a toilet and a sink. But the heavy metal door to the restroom was locked, with a sign posted on it saying that it was closed for the winter. There was a water fountain, but it too was shut off. I looked around, wondering what to do next. Then I saw a trail at the other end of the park that looked like it might lead down to the river. I followed the trail through some pine trees and brush until I came to a place hidden from both the road and the park, where I went off the path aways and found a place to go to the bathroom. Then I got back on the trail and kept walking until it ended at a steep, rocky bank.

I turned my feet sideways and half-slid down, crouching and hanging on to the strong grasses on either side so I didn't fall down. At the bottom of the bank, a long stretch of smooth gray rocks led out to the river. I walked out across the rocks, feeling every bump through my thin-soled shoes, to the edge of the river, where I knelt down and splashed my face with the icy water, then tried to use some of it to smooth my hair. When I put my hands down in the water, tiny brown minnows darted off in every direction. I took some of the water up in my cupped hands to rinse out my mouth and then drank a little, hoping it was safe and didn't have any diseases. It looked clean enough.

I was amazed at how clear the water was. I reckon that's why somebody named it the Clearwater. From high up, you can see the outline of each rock on the bottom even though the water must be several feet deep in the middle, and has a strong, swift current. Standing at the edge, I was surprised how loud it sounded: It was as loud as a freight train rushing past. The morning sun pricked out glints and highlights in the places where the water broke over the rocks. Looking downriver, I saw a man standing in the river up to his waist and flinging a long, thin stick back and forth, sending out loops of silver string that formed a figure eight in the air, then lay down in a soft, wavy line across the surface of the water. It reminded me of a clean sheet being snapped over a bed, then falling down gently over the top. I watched the line drift quietly along with the current and slowly sink. Then the man jerked the string up out of the water again, and flung it back and forth across the blue of the sky like before. It must be some kind of fishing, I thought, though it wasn't like any I'd seen before.

I walked upriver and away from the fisherman to find a place where I could be alone and sheltered from the breeze. Pretty soon I found a huge fallen log, bleached white by the sun, lying across the beach, with a flat enough rock right by it where I could sit and lean my back against the log and be somewhat out of the cold. I pulled my knees up underneath my dress and hugged them, and let the warm sun beat down on my face and arms and hair. Might as well sit here and wait a spell, I thought. Most of the shops wouldn't open for a while yet.

It sure was a pretty place. The sky was clear and sharp, just bluer than any blue I'd ever seen. Across the river and facing me, thick green trees marched straight up the hillside. When you looked at the mountains in the distance, the tops of the trees cut into the blue of the sky like the teeth of a giant, jagged saw. The clear colors, the crisp air and the dry, piney forest smell all added up to something completely new and different for me, and that was good. That was what I was looking for. Something completely different than what was.

I let myself doze in the morning sun. Let my thoughts drift like that silver line floating quiet down the river. Ever since I'd run away, I'd tried so hard to concentrate. Tried hard to believe God was with me, because my Momma had told me that was the case. Go with God, she said, gripping my face between her hands. He's gonna be with you. I can't go with you, but he will. And then she pressed my head hard into her bony chest, and we'd both cried. I never wanted her to let go, and when I sat there remembering it, I wanted to start crying all over again. Would I ever see my Momma again? I knew it wasn't likely.

As I sat there on that warm rock, drifting in and out of sleep, I saw a man come and sit right down next to me. Saw him or felt him,

I'm not sure, but suddenly he was there. I turned to look at him, and he reached out and brushed a piece of hair off my damp cheek, tucking it behind my ear. Then he ran the back of his fingers gently down my jaw, and he smiled. For a moment only I saw his eyes, deep and brown and full to overflowing with grief and joy and . . . understanding. He knew, and I knew that He knew. He understood every bit of it: All the things that had ever happened to me, even if no one else ever would. Then I started awake and I looked all around, but the man was gone. I wondered for a minute if it was just some silly girl's dream, but I knew it wasn't. Those eyes had seared themselves right into my soul. And I knew that this was something I could keep--a memory, more like a *knowing*, that I wasn't alone. Even if I couldn't see him most of the time, he was right there. I sat there in the sun for a while and savored it, trying to call it all back to mind, and make him come again. But after a while I knew that wasn't going to happen. You couldn't just make him come by willing it. And besides, the sun was climbing up toward the middle of the sky. It was high time to go try the shops for a job.

CHAPTER FOUR

I walked back up through the park and into town to the donut place, where I could get some breakfast. The windows were all steamed up from the crowd of people inside. Here goes nothin', I thought. I took a deep breath and pushed open the heavy glass door. All the noisy, lively talk stopped, and every eye in the shop turned and fixed itself on me. *Oh Jesus. Oh Jesus Jesus Jesus, I can't,* I thought.

But I did it anyway.

I let the door close behind me, and I went on in. The shop was filled with white men, some in shirts and ties and others in the loggers' uniform of a thick flannel shirt and denim. They sat watching me in stunned silence, and I wanted to turn and run right back out the door. But I didn't. I tried to pay them no mind. I tried not to be aware of each eye boring a hole into my back as I walked up to the counter, ordered a maple bar and a glass of milk, and slid my precious twenty dollar bill across the counter. My hands shook as I pocketed my change and grabbed my tray. But I looked the shopkeeper in the eye, and I asked him, in as smooth a voice as I could muster, "By the way Sir, are you hiring?"

The donut man stood stock still and gaping for what felt like a whole minute, he was so taken by surprise, before he managed to stammer, "Ummmm, no. I don't think we are."

"Thank you, Sir," I said, forcing myself to smile back at him. Forcing the great lump swelling up in my throat back down into its place. Then I carried my tray to an empty stool at the end of the bar. Slowly, the men started talking again, though regular, furtive glances kept on in my direction for as long as I sat there. I hadn't seen a single other black person since coming into town. Maybe that's what all the fuss was about.

I finished my maple bar, savoring each bit of frosting and each swallow of cold milk. A breakfast like that was a rare treat for me. And I needed time to gather my nerve to get up and walk out the shop past all those faces again, but finally I did it. I left the donut shop and walked the rest of the way up Main Street, then made a U-turn and came back down the other side. At every shop it was the same: A man or a woman, too stunned at first not to be rude and drop their jaw at me, quickly recovered and said no, they were sorry, but they weren't hiring. Conversations stopped and eyes followed me every step of the way, but I had decided back in the donut shop that no matter what, I was going to walk into each door with a smile and a how-do-you-do, and just keep going.

I met with no success that first day, but nobody was outright mean to me, or called out taunts and jeers like they did back home. The town was completely white. That was a shock to me. Of course I'd heard there were places were like this, but I hadn't realized Spring would be one of them. If I'd known, surely I would have picked somewhere else. But now that I'd used up all Momma's money to get here, it would just have to do.

After I'd tried every shop along Main Street, I walked back to the park by the river. Throughout the day, children had run and shouted and played on the swings and the metal slide, but it was deserted now. The afternoon sun hung low in the sky, and there was that soft yellow light you sometimes see about an hour before sunset, that turns everything it touches—the autumn leaves, the roofs of the buildings, the playground toys and the metal trim on all the cars—into gold. I sat on a bench and unwrapped the nut bar I'd bought for dinner. It had seemed the least expensive way to fill the emptiness that clawed at me from the inside. I felt faint with hunger, and so thirsty! I'd gone without food plenty of times, and never felt so hungry as this. Probably it was the baby, wanting his due. "Don't you worry," I spoke to it softly. "I'll find something for you and me. Jesus and me, we're going to take care of you."

As the golden light gave way to inky blue and finally dark, I hugged my arms around myself to keep from shivering. I wasn't too worried that I hadn't found work yet. I'd try again tomorrow, and by then maybe folks would've got over their surprise at seeing a black person, and a female at that, walking up and down their white sidewalks looking for work. Something would come up. Meanwhile,

I could bide my time. The janitor had hinted that I could keep sleeping in the church, and I still had nineteen dollars and thirty five cents left. If I was careful, that could last me for a week or even two. Anything might happen before then. Anything at all.

CHAPTER FIVE

The next morning, I was woken up by the sound of knocking. I sat up to face a tall, pale, dark haired man, dressed in a white shirt and a yellow striped tie. He was standing at the end of my pew and rapping on it with his knuckles, looking down at me as if I were a smudge on one of his fine white dishes, or a mouse shivering from as far back as possible in its hole in the wall. I sat up, smoothing the wrinkles from my dress, and faced him with as much dignity as I could muster, considering my disadvantaged situation. Behind the dark-haired man stood the janitor, wearing the same apron and shirt sleeves as the day before, holding his broom and looking down at the floor.

The man walked to the pew in front of me, then sat and turned to examine me. "What is your name?" he asked.

"My name is Flora Suzette Kenover," I said.

"Where do you come from?" he demanded.

I looked away, considering. I hadn't thought about what to tell people if they asked this, and I didn't know why he wanted to know. So I said simply, "East of here."

"You're a long ways from home, young lady," the man said sternly.

"Yes," I said.

"Don't be impertinent," he said, then he saw me stiffen up, and softened his voice a little. "Now, Miss Kenover, you can't keep sleeping in our church. People are beginning to talk. I don't know why you came to our town, but it's obvious you are a very young girl and you belong with your mother and father at home. I'll have to check with my deacon board, but I think I can say our church might be able to help with arrangements for your trip home. If you'll just give me your telephone number and address, I will contact your mother and father and tell them where you are. They're probably worried sick about you."

As the man talked, it was like alarm bells started ringing in my brain, and I felt more and more scared. I shook my head, saying, "No, no, I can't do that Sir. I can't. I won't."

"Why not?" the man asked, impatience edging into his voice.

Maybe I should have kept quiet and held my ground, or even just gotten up and walked out the door. But I was in a panic, and the words started pouring out of my mouth all on their own. "No, I can't do that Sir--I can't go home. If my Daddy finds out what state I'm in, he'll kill me. It was my Momma herself who helped me run away. My dad'd just kick me out again, or worse. You don't understand. " I could hear my voice rising, sounding hysterical. Fear was swirling in my brain, making me feel like I was going crazy. I twisted around to look in back of me, and decided to get up and run out the door, but the man reached out and grabbed my arm. Everything in me wanted to start screaming and kicking, but somehow I didn't. Somehow I could still hear the man's voice through the alarm bells in my head and the pounding in my ears.

"And what 'state' are you in? Why can't you go back?" the man said, demanding.

My heart was beating so hard I thought it would burst, and my breathing started to come too fast. The room swirled around me, and I felt like maybe I would faint, but the janitor slid into my pew then, and started talking to me in a soothing voice. He told me to put my head down between my knees and take deep breaths, and calm myself down. To my surprise, I was able to do it. The room stopped tilting and slid back into place, and I could feel the seat solid underneath me. The janitor was still talking in a soft, low voice. I didn't know exactly what he was saying, but whatever it was, it helped.

My heartbeat had slowed to almost normal, but I felt shaky and weak, and everything felt bleak and dead inside me. I looked up and both men were still there. The janitor was sitting at my side, and the other man was looking down at me. I wanted to sink right in to the earth. I felt embarrassed and ashamed, and I wished I was someplace far away. I looked down at the tiny life growing inside me, depending on me. There wasn't anything left to do now but to tell the truth, and trust that God would work it out somehow. I put my hand on my middle and I said, so softly the others had to lean forward to hear it, "I'm going to have a baby. Sir."

The dark haired man said harshly, "So. You're one of those kinds of girls. I might have suspected as much. In that case, you are particularly not welcome here, and it is my duty to escort you out immediately." He reached down to take my arm.

"No," I said softly, looking up in his eyes. The man stepped back, folded his arms across his chest, and looked away.

These men could do anything to me, I thought. They could call the police. They could make me go back. Somehow, I had to make them understand. I didn't mind so much about myself, but I had to try my best, to protect my baby. The baby was the only thing that mattered, and that focused me. "You don't understand," I said, and my voice was calm and clear. "I never wanted this baby. I never did anything to make it come. It was forced on me, there was nothing I could do to stop it. But now that I have it, it's my duty to take care of it. That's why I came to your town, and to your church. I needed to find someplace safe to raise my baby."

The dark haired man was still looking off out the window with his arms folded across his chest. Tapping his foot with impatience, but listening. The janitor was looking at me square and plain, understanding and sympathy in his eyes.

"And I am going to take care of it," I said, my voice growing stronger. "It's going to have everything it needs to be safe and happy and a success. You see, I had to run away to give my baby a chance. There's no future for me or for it back home."

The man looked down at me, frowning. Then he said, "Wait here," turned abruptly, and walked out of the room, each step sounding like a loud clap on the hard wood floor. The janitor was still looking at me and his eyes were so kind, I had to turn away, because his looking made me want to break down and cry. And this was no time to bawl like a baby, or lose my resolve. I had to be strong—strong so I could find a home for the baby. I put my head down in my hands and pressed my fingers hard against my eyes. Oh Jesus, Jesus, I begged silently. Find us a home, Jesus—a real home! And make me strong enough to take care of this baby, because you know I'm just a girl. Not a woman yet. Just a girl. Jesus.

CHAPTER SIX

I waited, sitting in that pew, for half an hour. I badly needed to find the toilet, but decided I'd better just stay put. At last I heard the clapping of the Reverend's heels on the floorboards again, and the quiet shuffle of the janitor's steps behind. I tried to take deep breaths and stay calm. I pressed my hands together hard in my lap to stop them from shaking. And something deep inside me was praying all the time, please God please God please God.

"Well, Miss . . . Miss . . .", the Reverend said, from the end of my pew.

"Kenover," I said.

"Well, Miss Kenover, it seems that our janitor and his wife will be able to take you in, temporarily. I hope that you are grateful."

He looked both nervous and relieved, and when he swallowed I could see the Adam's apple move up and then down his thin neck. He was looking down at me, expecting a reply. From behind him, the janitor gave a friendly smile and a nod.

"Yes, Sir. I am very grateful," I said.

"All right then. I'll leave you two to discuss arrangements. I need to go and attend to church business."

When the pale, dark haired man finally left my whole body sighed with relief, and I felt like I could breathe again. The janitor said kindly, "Come along then, and I'll take you to the house. Do you have a suitcase?"

"No," I said.

"No bags?" he said. "Well that makes it right simple then." Then the janitor walked to the door and held it open, so I could walk through like some princess in a fairy tale. "By the way," he said at the bottom of the steps, holding out his hand, "I'm Jake Foxworthy. You can call me Jake."

I took his hand and shook it up and then down. I'd never done such a thing before, but I'd seen others do it, so I knew what to do. Where I came from, no white man would ever extend his hand to a black man, never mind a woman. The white people never even met your eyes. They looked away from you, and sometimes even crossed the street or stepped off to the side if you came too close. But I walked next to the janitor all the way back down Main Street, which felt awful strange. I felt like I should walk behind him, but when I tried, he only slowed down and matched his walking to mine. We passed several shops and people stared at us the whole way, but he didn't seem to notice. Then we turned and went down a few other streets until we came to a small trailer park. We walked one, two, three, four plots down to a single-wide aluminum mobile home, neat and white with a big turquoise stripe running along the side. The janitor went up the steps of a small wooden porch and held the door open for me again.

I found myself standing in a rectangular room lined with wooden walls. There was a sofa and two cushioned chairs with colorful crocheted blankets folded over the backs. Shelves on the walls were crowded with all kinds of vases, knick knacks and photographs in frames. The corner of the room turned like a big L, where there was a round table covered with a cloth and four matching wooden chairs. Coming from that side of the room was a small woman wearing a simple cotton dress a lot like mine, except she had stockings and nice shoes to go with it and an apron tied over the top. The woman was wiping her hands on the apron and smiling. "I'm Janice Foxworthy," she said, holding out her hand. "And I'm so glad you've come to stay for a few days."

"I'm Flora," I managed to stammer, and for the second time I shook a white person's hand. She turned to her husband and asked, "Did Jake bring all your things? We can put them in your room, and I'll show you around."

"I didn't bring any things," I said.

"No things?" she replied, her tiny, plucked eyebrows darting up in surprise. "Well, follow me then, and I'll show you our home."

Mrs. Foxworthy seemed to flutter from place to place like a moth, gesturing this way and that as she talked, opening the doors for the bathroom and a narrow closet full of towels. "The boys are grown and gone now, so you can have Tom's room," she said, walking in to one of the rooms.

I stepped in and looked around. There was a double bed covered with a soft quilt full of colors. The linoleum floor had a soft, shaggy rug right next to the bed. The closet doors were open, and space had been cleared for the clothes I didn't have. There was a wooden dresser with six drawers, and a painted blue desk with a matching chair. Framed pictures hung on the walls, and there were real draperies on the windows. And it was all for me. I sat down on the bed, stunned and quiet. Never in my whole life had I slept in a room as nice as this. It felt like I was in some kind of dream. I even wondered if maybe I'd fainted because of not having any breakfast yet. I'd heard things like that could happen when a person was going to have a baby.

Mrs. Foxworthy stopped her cheerful, breathless talking and looked down at me with concern. "Is everything all right?" she asked.

I looked up at her, afraid to say a word in case the strange spell of goodness I'd somehow stepped into break, and fly apart into pieces. "Oh Ma'am," I said. "I never knew how other people lived before. I never knew people could be so kind before."

And then, despite the strong resolve I'd kept for days and

days, tears started streaming down my face. I was overwhelmed by the kindness of these people that I'd hardly even met. I wanted to shrink into the earth for shame, but I couldn't help it. All those pent up tears from the past three months just started flooding up and out of me, and once they started, there was just no stopping them.

Mrs. Foxworthy was sitting down next to me in an instant. "There, there, Dear . . . there, there. It's all right. You just cry yourself out now. It's all right. It must have been such a long trip for you, and no idea what you'd find at the end of it. Really, I can't even imagine!"

I cried for a long time. Even after all my tears had run out, I just sat there, letting my head rest against the woman's shoulder, letting her pat and rub my back. When at last I looked up, Mrs. Foxworthy asked gently, "Is there anything you would like, Flora Dear, before I make breakfast?"

I blew my nose out with the tissue she gave me. Then I nodded and said, "Yes, Ma'am. I need to use the toilet."

"Of course you do!" Mrs. Foxworthy said, jumping up. "And I bet you'd like a nice warm bath, too. You can use our soap and shampoo, and I'll get you some fresh towels. You can just leave your dress and underthings outside the door, and I'll wash them. In the meantime, you can borrow something of mine. I declare, we're about the same size, except for the height of course!" And she became a fluttering moth again, flitting out the bedroom and down the hall, busy as a bird.

I waited on the bed while Mrs. Foxworthy found some

clothes and ran a bath. Then I crept quietly into the bathroom. After folding my things and setting them carefully outside the door, I stepped into the tub and laid myself full down. I'd never had a deep, warm bath like that before. Back home it was an inch or two of cold water, and you sat up on the side and did your business as fast as you could. And that was when the water wasn't shut off. I closed my eyes and felt the water swishing up around my ears. It made everything sound strange and close. I could hear the sound of my blood thumping in my ears, and the growling of my empty belly. I wondered if any of the sounds were from the baby.

I lay like that for a long time, just feeling the warm water lapping up all around me. I felt peaceful and calm, and all emptied out somehow. Like a clean white page with no writing on it, and no smudges or wrinkles. Then I sat up and washed everything twice with the soap and washcloth they'd put out for me, scrubbing to get off all the dirt from the past week. The shampoo for my hair smelled like flowers, and there were two bottles, one that said shampoo, and one that said conditioner. I'd never heard of conditioner before, so I carefully read the back of the bottle and tried it. It made my hair feel a little bit softer.

I got out, drained the tub and got dressed, and then scrubbed out the dirty ring left in the tub. I'd always hated being dirty, but sometimes a person just didn't have any choice. But after that bath I felt clean and new as a newborn baby. It was almost like a baptism, I thought. A baptism into a new place, and a new way of life. I still didn't know what would happen to me in the weeks ahead, but when

I was laying there in the warm water, something had come inside me to replace at least some of the fear, and that was hope. Hope, and love, and all the goodness in that little trailer. Part of me was afraid to trust it, but there it was right in front of me and plain to see, so I let myself take some of it in. It was a new day for Flora Suzette Kenover. And I decided there in that bathroom to stay in Spring, and no matter what happened, to keep walking forward. To keep on stepping on through.

CHAPTER SEVEN

I had two helpings of eggs, and something called hash browns, which were potatoes that were grated and then fried in a pan until they were crispy on all the edges. They were absolutely delicious. As soon as I set my fork and knife down on my plate, Mrs. Foxworthy sprang up from the table to wash and rinse. Jake had already left to go back to the church and finish his morning's work. I watched Mrs. Foxworthy flutter from place to place in the tidy kitchen. I was still just trying to believe it all. I felt caught in some world of pretend, the kind I used to read about when I would sneak off to the library in our town and read for hours on end. I kept expecting all the strange and wonderful things to snap back into their usual places—for the cozy, bright room to fade into the background, and real life, cold and hard and gray, to come and take its place. But there was Mrs. Foxworthy, sitting down now across the table from me, wrapping her tiny hands around a steaming cup of coffee.

"Have you seen much of our little town yet?" she asked

brightly.

I nodded and answered, "I've been up and down Main Street, and into all the shops. I'm looking for a job."

Mrs. Foxworthy laughed out loud. "I don't imagine you had much luck."

"No, Ma'am, I didn't. Most folks just dropped their jaw when they saw me. But I'll find something."

Mrs. Foxworthy put her chin in her hand, looked at me, and said, "People here aren't used to seeing a girl like you. I've lived in Spring all my life, and I've never known a black family to live here. You've certainly taken us all by surprise."

We were quiet for a time, looking out the sliding door next to the table onto a small deck and yard. Seeds had been scattered along the railing of the deck, and a number of birds were flying down to eat. The bigger birds squawked and puffed out their chests, and chased the smaller birds away. But as soon as they bent their heads down to eat, the little birds flew right back in. A steep hillside loomed straight up from the last trailer in the row, and the side yards were all littered with dry brown needles. There sure were a lot of pine trees in this place. It was a cold day, and I heard the wind whistling loud through the trees. I felt thankful to be sitting inside, out of the weather.

Mrs. Foxworthy stirred her coffee, and spoke into the quiet. "But maybe you needn't worry about finding work just yet. When a little time passes and people get used to the idea, some of the ladies in town might have things you can help out with. For the time being, you can stay with us."

"I don't know how to thank you," I said. "You and Mr. Foxworthy are so kind."

"Oh, posh," said Mrs. Foxworthy. "It's not such a big deal. It's just what people should do. Jake and I talk all the time about how quiet and lonely it is now, with the boys all grown and gone. Tom, our oldest, works down in Boise, and our younger boy George just got a job halfway across the country. Who knows but that you've been sent here because we needed the company!"

I could only blink at her. Like so many things that day, it was too much to take in.

Mrs. Foxworthy sprang up again, taking her mug to the sink and scrubbing it inside and out as she talked. "I thought we might go into town and get you some clothes. You're going to need a warm coat and some socks for sure. And maybe another dress and some underthings as well."

"Oh!" I said, jumping up and reaching into the pocket of my borrowed dress. "I have money! I was going to save it for food, but maybe now I could use it for clothes instead."

"How much money do you have?"

"Nineteen dollars and thirty five cents."

"That should be enough to get a few things," Mrs. Foxworthy said, "And I can help out if it doesn't quite cover it. Just for today you can borrow this old coat of mine. I'm afraid it's not the latest style, but it'll do for today."

Mrs. Foxworthy held out a woolen coat, and I slipped my arms through the sleeves. It was silky on the inside, and had fur around the neck and cuffs. My wrists stuck out the sleeves like stalks of celery, but the coat was soft and warm. Mrs. Foxworthy handed me hat and a pair of gloves to put on as well.

As we walked into town, Mrs. Foxworthy introduced me to several people on the street. Most of the folks nodded and smiled at me, and no one was outright rude. Mrs. Foxworthy bustled from store to store, knowing exactly where to go for each item, and greeting all the shopkeepers by name. There was a tiny J. C. Penney store with a few things like socks and underwear in the front, but it was mostly just a place to order out of a catalog. There was a shoe store called Hermann's, and a trendy clothing store for ladies called The Mode. The last place we went to was a kind of general store that had a little bit of everything, including clothes.

We bought a navy blue wool coat, a loose plaid jumper and a turtleneck to wear underneath it, a thick button up sweater, a pair of brown slacks with buttons along the side to make the waist bigger as the baby grew, and a loose fitting pink blouse that went with the slacks. We also bought sturdy leather shoes, knee high socks, seven pairs of underwear and two bras. The coat used up most of my money, and I said I could wait until I found a job to buy more. But

Mrs. Foxworthy wouldn't hear of it, and said that no house guest of hers would go shivering through the winter with a thin summer dress and no socks or decent shoes while she was able to do something about it. All along the way Mrs. Foxworthy told me about how she'd never had a daughter to buy pretty clothes for, and how boys' clothes weren't any fun to shop for at all, so I should let her have the pleasure just this once. Before long I was too worn down by so many new and wonderful things, each one following so close on the heels of the last, to say any more. The enthusiasm of Mrs. Foxworthy was like a swift flowing creek, and after a while, I just let the current sweep me up and carry me away.

I was too overwhelmed to make choices, or know what I liked. Shopping for new clothes was not something I'd ever done before. I'm not sure where Momma got our clothes, but it certainly wasn't at a store. Hand-me-downs from cousins or friends in the neighborhood would be my guess. So Mrs. Foxworthy recruited the sales ladies to give their opinions. They brought out item after item for me to look at and admire, and I tried them all on. I felt vain and foolish, like some kind of spoiled movie star, but I didn't want to spoil their fun. I tried to say something when they asked my opinion, but for the most part I just let matters take their course, and let Mrs. Foxworthy and the others choose what was best.

When we'd finished our shopping and were leaving the last store, my eye lit on a knitted scarf and hat set hanging on a rack near the front door. I reached out to touch the fine, soft stuff. I'd never felt anything like it. I'd had a scarf once, knit out of thick, stiff wool, and it itched like the devil. I hid it under a bush one day walking to school, figuring it was better to be cold. But this scarf was nothing like that. Mrs. Foxworthy snatched up the scarf and hat and the matching gloves as well, and headed back to the register without even looking at the tag. Then she returned and handed the bag to me, saying, "All this time I've been waiting for you to pick out something you really liked. I finally caught you!"

Speechlessly, I took the bag.

We stopped to eat lunch at a restaurant I'd gone in to the day before. There were cushioned booths along the front windows and up one side. A waitress met us at the front door and led us to a booth, then handed me a big padded menu.

I'd never been to a restaurant before, so I watched Mrs. Foxworthy carefully for clues about what to do. The menu had so many choices. When the waitress came and asked for our order, I shook my head helplessly, so Mrs. Foxworthy ordered for both of us. Soon after, the waitress came back carrying two fancy white plates with chicken salad sandwiches on them. Each sandwich had been cut into four triangles, and tiny wooden sticks with sparkly stuff on top were stuck into the bread. There was a frilly piece of lettuce underneath, and a sliced pickle spread out like a fan on one side. There was also a little bag of potato chips for each of us, and tall glasses of Coca Cola with ice floating and tinkling on top. I ate slowly and carefully, washing down each bite of sandwich with a tiny sip of cola, and wiping my mouth carefully with the corner of my napkin after each bite. I'd put my napkin in my lap like I saw Mrs.

Foxworthy do, which didn't seem very practical, but apparently that's what you do at a restaurant. It was the best sandwich I ever had. I wondered how much it had all cost, but Mrs. Foxworthy picked up the bill too fast for me to see.

We returned to the trailer, arms loaded with bags. I went to my room and carefully arranged my socks and underwear in a drawer, and hung up my pants, my jumper and sweater, and the two shirts in the closet. I lined up my shoes on the floor underneath. Then I stood there and tried to make myself believe all these beautiful, brand new things were mine. If you put your face into the closet, the clothes even smelled new. Then suddenly I felt dizzy, and in fact the room seemed to start spinning around. Mrs. Foxworthy walked past and saw me hanging onto the side of the dresser. She came in and told me to lie down, and even folded down the bedding for me to get in. I took off my shoes and crawled inside the crisp, flower printed sheets, put my head on the soft pillow, and didn't wake up again until the room was pitch dark, and it was well past the normal time for supper.

CHAPTER EIGHT

I wanted to make myself as useful as possible, but I had a lot to learn. I'd never seen a washing machine or dryer before, and it seemed like a miracle how clean the clothes came out. I'd heard of vacuum cleaners, but I'd never used one. Mrs. Foxworthy helped me find some books about how to raise babies from the library, and she was also teaching me to knit and crochet, so I could make some things for the baby. She was a quick teacher and not over-patient, but I caught on pretty quick.

Evenings after the dishes were done, the three of us sat in the living room, Mrs. Foxworthy and I with our projects, and Mr. Foxworthy with a book or newspaper. Sometimes we played cards, or I would play checkers with Mr. Foxworthy. Once in a while we watched a program on television, but most of the time it was just quiet. I liked the quiet best. Back home, it was never quiet—there was always someone caterwauling, someone yelling in the street, and cars and sirens all through the night. Always plenty of noise inside as well as out. So the quiet was a relief to my mind. For the first time in my life, I felt like I could think my own thoughts without being interrupted, or having to stay on guard for what might happen next. After a while I realized I felt happy. I'd never felt that before, just quiet on the inside and happy.

At first Mr. and Mrs. Foxworthy asked a lot of questions. But I had decided that I just didn't want to talk about my former life. What had happened had happened—it couldn't be undone. I felt sad sometimes in the privacy of my own little room, and I talked about it and sometimes even cried about it with Jesus. But in general it seemed best to just keep putting one foot in front of the other, and walk forward. Before long the Foxworthys stopped asking questions, and seemed to accept me as I was. And the three of us settled into a routine that felt as natural as though it had always been.

The first month I was in Spring, I slept more than I'd ever slept in my life, going to bed early and waking up shamefully late. The nights were so quiet, and it felt so safe there. My belly started to swell almost immediately after I arrived. I was so skinny that pretty soon, the baby stuck out in front of me like a big round ball. When the baby started to kick and move I could see it, moving like a tiny mountain peak across the middle of my dress. Mr. and Mrs. Foxworthy were as thrilled as if it were one of their own grandchildren.

As the baby grew, it kicked more and more. It seemed as soon as I would sit or lie down to rest a little, the pummeling would begin, and I would even cry out as the baby found its way beneath my rib cage, or stuck a limb down into my hip. My hips and back ached terribly sometimes, but the doctor told me that was normal, because things had to stretch out for when the baby came. Mrs. Foxworthy borrowed some more maternity clothes from the Pastor's wife, who had just had a baby boy. And all of us waited, with eagerness and nervousness as well, the day the little brute would kick its way out into the world.

Every Sunday we went to church. Mrs. Foxworthy would flutter about the sanctuary, squeezing hands and patting arms and talking to every person she met. She seemed to know everyone, and she introduced me to them all. Jake stood quiet at her side, and sometimes he winked or smiled at me on the sly at the awkwardness of other people. A few times when a person was especially rude, he even squeezed my hand. Who were these people, I thought—who had taken me into their home, and stood by me even when they were snubbed by their own white friends? I just couldn't understand it, and one Sunday on the way to church I told them I'd be just fine sitting in the back so they could talk to their friends without me in the way. But they told me they would never consider such a thing, and neither should I. We talked a lot that day at lunch, about how black people should be treated as equals because they were created equal by God. This was a new and different thought for me. It wasn't the world I'd grown up in, and always known. It was true in that, according to my observations, white people weren't any more intelligent or morally superior than black people. Whether they were black or white, some people were good and some were bad. Some were quick and some were slow. But it still seemed forward to think in this new way. It felt all wrong to me, as if I was taking liberties I shouldn't.

I tried my best to observe the folks around me and fit in, and never say or do anything that would bring any embarrassment or shame to the Foxworthys. It was a different world, among these white folks. Most people didn't say what they really meant. They spoke one thing with their mouths, another thing entirely with their faces and eyes. I couldn't wrap my mind around it, so most of the time I kept my mouth shut and let Mrs. Foxworthy do the talking. I knew if I was anything, I was plain spoken, and I was no good at putting on airs. I wished there were one or two other black people to talk to, so I could learn how things were in this new place—what was expected of me, and how I should act. But there weren't. Except for the Foxworthys, I was on my own. They were the kindest people in the world, but they couldn't be expected to understand how different everything was for me, or how alone I felt at times.

But Jesus knew. I felt him there right next to me, much of the time. Times when I didn't, I just kept reminding myself that it was true. My Momma told me that even if he hides his face for a while, he'll show it again, sure enough. She said that's just the way he tests our faith. If it weren't for knowing that, I don't know what I would have done. Maybe run away at some point to a bigger city where there were more people like me. It would have been a hard life, but it would have felt more familiar. And maybe I could have found a friend or two my own age, or a neighborhood where I fit in. But I felt very clearly that the Lord had brought me to Spring, so I stayed put. I also thought my baby would have a better chance to grow up wholesome here in Spring than in a big city.

I'd never been to a white church before coming to Spring. The whole place seemed dull and lifeless. Nobody clapped or moved around when they sang; instead everyone stood still as a post and looked down into their hymnals, even when they already knew the song. I held my hymnal in front of me with both hands and stared down at it, and stood up and sat down with everyone else. Most of the time I couldn't make heads or tails out of anything the Preacher said. His explanations of Greek words and ancient history put my head in a spin. The sermons were nothing like the lively stories I'd always looked forward to hearing in my church back home. Ever since our first meeting, Reverend Pinehurst had been distant and cold. Even if I was from a more humble station in life, I thought, a Reverend shouldn't treat someone in his church that way. As far as I was could tell, he had all the marks of one of the Scribes or Pharisees that Jesus was always warning everyone about.

I'd had little in the way of school education, at least little of much quality. But I did know my Bible. Thanks to Momma, I'd grown up going to church and hearing all the Bible stories. Momma couldn't read, but she knew those stories by heart, and she told them to us kids in her own embellished style on nights when Daddy was away. Once I'd learned to read, there was nothing Momma liked better than having me read out loud to her from the Bible. I missed my church back home—the clapping and the swaying, and everybody singing as loud as he or she could possibly sing. Life was hard—everyone knew that. But on Sundays you could forget about that for a little while. Sundays were like a big party. They were a little taste of heaven while we were still down here suffering on the earth, Momma said. But this white church was nothing like a party.

So many good things had happened to me since I'd arrived in this tiny little town, I thought I could just keep quiet and endure it, for Mr. and Mrs. Foxworthy's sake. I couldn't help wondering what they got out of the whole routine. But maybe all the white churches were like this, and they didn't know any different.

CHAPTER NINE

One Sunday morning, after the Prayer of Invocation and the Offering, the Hymns and the reading of that morning's passage, Reverend Pinehurst walked up and took his place behind the pulpit. He stood there longer than usual, blinking at the audience like a great big goldfish, then took a deep breath, opened up his big leather Bible, and began to speak.

"Today, in place of our regular sermon series, I am going to address a matter that has recently come up within our body. The theme of my message is the holiness of God and the purity of Christ and his saints, and how we as his saints are to deal with the foreigner who comes into our midst." He took another deep breath, and looked around nervously. Then he looked down and read from his notes.

"Come out from among them and be separate! So says the word of God. And we can see his hand of providence stretching all the way back to Genesis, all the way back to the sons of Noah, when he chose one son for himself, and placed the other under a curse. When the righteous brother Shem was given favor, whereas his brother Ham received condemnation. This curse has remained upon the race of Ham throughout the ages, and we can see with our own eyes and in our own nation that the white man has thrived and prospered, and that, both biblically and historically, the black man, descended from Canaan, the son of Ham, has been destined to serve him."

Reverend Pinehurst stopped then and looked up. I heard Mrs. Foxworthy suck in her breath with a small cry that sounded like pain, and I felt Mr. Foxworthy stiffen next to me. The two of them looked at each other in shock. Mrs. Foxworthy reached across and grabbed my hand. I could feel every eye in the church boring down into me, and my face burned hot with shame. Then Mr. Foxworthy said, quietly but distinctly, "You don't have to listen to this, Flora. We're leaving." He got up, and nodded at me to get up too, so I did. Mrs. Foxworthy bustled behind us, gathering our things. I walked in front of them, out the pew and down the center aisle to the doors in back, my eyes glued to the floorboards. The whole congregation started whispering and talking as we left, and behind my back I could hear Reverend Pinehurst trying to speak over the din. "If I could just have your attention please . . . I fear you all are misinterpreting what I was going to say. If everyone will turn just back around, and keep listening . . ."

We walked back to the trailer in the stillness of a small town Sunday morning, our backs warmed by the spring sun. It was an absolutely beautiful, blue sky day. The birds twittered and sang, calling out to each other across the road. Mrs. Foxworthy was exclaiming, "The nerve of that man! How could he say such things with you sitting right there in the room? How horrible that must have been for you, Flora—Horrible!" Mr. Foxworthy was silent except for one comment when we were most of the way home. "Janice, we're never going back to that church again."

"Of course we aren't!" Mrs. Foxworthy said. "I absolutely agree with you!"

I walked with Mrs. Foxworthy's tiny arm tucked into mine, hot tears spilling down my cheeks. I thought of them making splotches in the dusty road, a trail marking our way home, like in that story with the boy and the bread crumbs. When we reached the trailer, Jake held the door open for us and then said, "I'm going for a walk. You two go on and eat lunch without me."

Mrs. Foxworthy nodded and pulled me inside. "He's angry," she said, as she hung up our sweaters, and then walked me over to the couch. "My Jake doesn't get angry often, but when he does, he wants to walk by the river and cool off."

She sat next to me on the sofa and watched anxiously as the tears kept running down my face. She got me a handkerchief and I buried my face in it, trying to smother the crying. I just couldn't look at that good woman. Such an awful mixture of emotions was churning inside me—anger and shame, and even hate. Hate for that awful Preacher man who had singled me out, when I had been trying so hard to fit in.

"Oh Flora—I am so sorry. I'm sorry we ever took you to that place. We had guessed some of Reverend Pinehurst's views, but I never dreamed he would be so thoughtless as to single you out right like that. I thoughts things would blow over eventually. That maybe if he had time to get to know you a bit, he would come around. But of course it will never be that way now."

I sat, twisting the handkerchief in my hands, staring straight ahead. Then I said, "Do other people think those things—that I'm part of a curse, because I'm black? Do you?"

"Goodness sakes, no!" said Mrs. Foxworthy. "It seems to me that some people take little bits out of the Bible, lift them out, and make them say whatever they want them to say. Reverend Pinehurst is full of pride, so he looks at the Scriptures, and that's what he sees. And then he went to seminary somewhere in the South, so maybe he's repeating things he was taught there. I've read the Bible for years, and I've never seen any such thing."

"Me neither," I said, looking down at the handkerchief in my lap. "I must be such an embarrassment to you. I bet everyone talks about you and Mr. Foxworthy behind your backs, because of me."

"You mustn't think that way, Flora," Mrs. Foxworthy said. "Jake and I have you with us because we want you here. As far as what others think or say, we can't change that. We only have to do what we feel is right. And try and be kind and forgive, like Jesus did. They hated him too, you know. He knows all about prejudice and hate."

"He does?" I looked up.

"Oh yes! They called him illegitimate—a Bastard even, if you will excuse my language. Not a nice word at all. When he was alive not one of them understood who he really was. His own people, the Jews, rejected him and had him killed. Even his own family, his mother and brothers, didn't understand. They thought he was crazy, and they all came down one day when he was preaching to try and make him come home. He practically had to disown them. Jesus lived with those things all the time."

I nodded, remembering. Those things were in the Bible, though I'd never given them much notice before. If Jesus could put up with people hating him and still forgive them, maybe I could, too. But he sure wasn't lying when he said it wasn't the easy road. It would have been the easiest thing in the world to hate Reverend Pinehurst right then, and start hating all the others too—the whole sea of white faces that had muttered and whispered behind my back as I walked out of that church. But I knew I had to fight those feelings, and forgive. No matter what I felt inside, that was the right thing to do. Mrs. Foxworthy and I talked about what happened later that week, and she told me that most people are silly and weak sometimes. Most of them don't mean any harm, not really. They're just looking around at all the others, and trying to fit in. When I thought things over I decided she was probably right, and that helped me to forgive.

The next Monday morning at 8:55 am, Mr. Foxworthy set out for the church with a carefully typed letter of resignation in his hand, which also included a request to withdraw his and his wife's long standing membership at the First Baptist Church of Spring. When I protested that he didn't need to give up his job, he said, "Oh, we can do without the money. I just took the job to keep myself useful. We're all set up to retire."

"I don't want you to do it because of me," I told him.

"Maybe it was coming around anyway. Ever since this new Reverend came, things haven't been the same. Old Reverend Baxter now, he was different. He was a real man of God."

From that point on, we attended Mass at the Catholic Church on the other side of the river with Mr. Foxworthy's mother. Father Johnston, the Parish priest, seemed genuinely happy to have us come. When he met me, he took one of my hands in both of his own and held it, and he looked right in my eyes, which hardly anyone ever did. I felt welcomed and taken in—not ashamed or put down at all. I'm sure he heard what had happened across the river at First Baptist, but he never mentioned it.

"I think I like that place," I said, as we rumbled home in Mr. Foxworthy's truck after my first Mass. "All the bending and kneeling and making signs seems strange. But I like it."

"I know, it does feel rather awkward at first, though of course I've been to Mass many times with Jake's mother. But maybe it doesn't matter much," said Mrs. Foxworthy. "Father Johnston has always been welcoming to us, even though we went to the other church. And he's always doing kind things for people. That's the true mark of a Christian, I think. You know Jake's father grew up Baptist, but his mother was a Catholic. They went to the Baptist church while Jake's father was alive, then after he died, she just switched right back! And the two of them always got along very well, which I suppose is quite unusual, though it shouldn't be. I really don't think God is as particular about these things as we humans can be. He seems to show up in both places."

I had to think about that. I didn't know much about Catholics, and I'd never met a priest before. I wondered what Momma would think of it all. But Momma would not have liked the First Baptist church for sure. I decided she'd probably just be happy that I was going to church at all.

CHAPTER TEN

It was a warm afternoon in early May, and the little trailer had started to heat up. Mrs. Foxworthy had just returned from the storage shed with a fan, and was busy cleaning the blades and setting it up so the breeze pointed the right way. I'd been rolling out a crust for a pie when I stopped, pressed my hands against the lower part of my back, and said, "My back has been hurting me all day."

Mrs. Foxworthy gave me a sharp look, and then, wiping her hands on a towel, she came over and took my arm to lead me away from the counter. "I really think you should lie down for a bit, Dear. I can finish up here. Maybe we ought to call the doctor."

"Oh no, you don't need to do that. I'm sure I'll be just . . ." Then suddenly I stopped and bent over double with pain. I might have fallen right down if Mrs. Foxworthy hadn't been there. She eased me down to the kitchen floor and helped me lean my back against the cupboards.

The pain hit me like a Mack truck—a full frontal assault, with contractions coming only a few minutes apart. Mrs. Foxworthy went over to the phone and stayed there for a long time, watching me with a worried expression and asking me questions from the doctor. But I was in no state to talk. My eyes were squeezed tight against the pain, and I started shaking all over.

Mrs. Foxworthy hung up the phone and came and knelt down next to me. "The doctor is going to come over here, he thinks there might not be enough time to drive to the hospital. It's over an hour away, you know. He said I should just try to make you as comfortable as I can. So hold on tight, I'm going to fetch some pillows and things. Then I'm going to call Jake so he can pray."

I nodded an answer, because I couldn't speak. The pain had completely taken me over. I felt like there was a great, shadowed man standing over me, looking down. And everything around me— all the safe, familiar things—seemed to fade back and out of reach. And I felt horribly, terrifyingly alone.

Mrs. Foxworthy came back with pillows, a light blanket, and towels. "I'm sorry about this floor," she said, as she put some towels down and helped me lie on my side, shifting a pillow under my head. "It isn't the most comfortable place, but things are going to get pretty messy, so I think it's best if we stay in here. For goodness sake, I'm glad I just mopped!"

And then Mrs. Foxworthy sat down next to me on the floor, stroking my forehead and saying soft things that I couldn't really hear through the pain. But hearing her voice helped me remember that I wasn't alone after all, and the huge shadowy man I'd felt standing over me before faded away. Having her with me helped me to focus and not go crazy, so later I could do what I needed to do. When the doctor came, Mrs. Foxworthy didn't leave my side. She called out to him that the door was open, and he could come in. The baby was ready to come almost immediately, though the pushing seemed to last for an eternity. But just when I didn't think I would ever get the baby out, he came.

He was a sturdy, meaty fellow, with a head as round as a basketball and fists balled up tight to take on the world. His cry when he came seemed to reach me from someplace far away. It broke into my world, and it seemed like the loudest thing I'd ever heard. I would have laughed out loud at the sound of it if it hadn't hurt too much to laugh. Mrs. Foxworthy washed the baby and wrapped him in a flannel blanket while the doctor finished up on me. Then she brought him over. When they propped me up against some pillows and put him in my arms, he looked up at me with a look of pure, questioning intensity.

As the doctor and Mrs. Foxworthy bustled back and forth cleaning up, I gazed down at him. "Oh, I know you," I said softly, putting my pinkie finger in his little clenched fist, and dancing it back and forth. "You want your due. Just like you've always done. You're ready for the whole world served up on a silver platter, and right now. And you know I'd give it to you if I could. I'd give you everything I have." I whispered this last part into his ear, so the others wouldn't hear. It was my promise to him and to God, like a blessing. And I felt a powerful surge of love rise up in me. I pictured fire coming out of me and forming an impenetrable ring around the two of us, sitting there on that kitchen floor. I knew I would do whatever it took for this baby to grow up wholesome and live a good life, to grow up and bless God. Out of the darkness of his conception, Jesus and me were going to forge something good.

But sitting there on the kitchen floor, I felt the Lord cluing me in that it was going to be one long fight. It wasn't going to be like the commercials I'd seen on TV for diapers or baby formula, with a woman in a long white dress sitting in a rocking chair cuddling her baby, and soothing music playing in the background. There was going to be very little that was peaceful or sweet about it. I was glad that if that was the case, I had fair warning. It was one of those times I felt the Lord right there next to me, so close I could have just turned my head and talked to him. I didn't of course, because the doctor and Mrs. Foxworthy might have thought I was crazy. But when the Lord came and sat with me like that for one flash of a minute, somehow he also let me know that whatever came in days ahead, I would never be alone.

The doctor took my temperature, then spent a long time giving Mrs. Foxworthy directions at the door. I couldn't believe it was over. The birth felt like it happened in some fuzzy, unreal time and place separate from real life. Later, when I sat all cleaned up and propped up in my own comfortable bed, Mrs. Foxworthy helped me aim the baby at my breast and have him suck. From the first, he drank with such ferocity that Mrs. Foxworthy said she'd never seen the likes of it, and that at least I shouldn't ever have to wonder if he was getting enough to eat. After a few minutes the baby wore himself out and fell fast asleep, his tiny, scrunched up face relaxing only a little as he dropped off. Mrs. Foxworthy took him and put him in the bassinet that she had set up right next to my bed. "I'm going to go do some cleaning up now, and let you rest," she said. "You'd better get some sleep while you can."

I nodded, still thinking about everything. Just before the door closed, I said, "Mrs. Foxworthy?"

"Yes?"

"I . . . I just wanted to thank you for being there with me. I can't imagine what it would have been like if I was all alone." I shuddered just from thinking of it.

"I'm glad I could be there. No woman should have to go through childbirth alone, God forbid! But it's over now, and you don't ever have to go through it again, if you don't want to. Or who knows, maybe someday you will! Now get some rest while you can," she said. "Your boy will be crying for you soon enough."

"Okay," I said, and I eased my sore self slowly down the bed. I didn't feel sleepy in the least. Scenes of the birth kept replaying themselves over and over in my head. And here was this tiny, living person, all wrapped up and snuffling away just a few inches from me. Everything had happened so fast. I could hardly remember what the doctor on call had looked like, the sound of his voice, or him being there at all.

In the space of a few hours, my world had changed. I was a mother, and I was just a girl. The two ideas would not fit together in my mind. They were like two jigsaw puzzle pieces with ends that don't match up, no matter how hard you press them together. Or maybe more like pieces from two completely different puzzles. I couldn't imagine falling asleep when everything felt so strange. But I must have done, because I woke several hours later in a darkened room to the baby's cry.

CHAPTER ELEVEN

I wanted to name my baby something significant, something that said he had a different heritage than my own, so I asked Father Johnston for some good ideas. He told me several stories of saints in the church, and even gave me a book about the saints that I could take home and read. I decided to name my baby Augustine Francis Kenover, but from the beginning his nickname was Gus. I had him baptized in the Catholic way, and Father Johnston spoke blessings over him, with Mr. and Mrs. Foxworthy, who had officially agreed to be the godparents, standing beside. Mrs. Foxworthy made a special lunch afterward, and Father Johnston and a few others came over to celebrate. The only sad part was when I thought about my Momma, and wished she could have been there. But I was happy and grateful for the love that surrounded me. I knew that the birth of baby Gus could have been a very different scene without all these kind people who had done so much to help me out.

Right from the start, Gus was a full bodied, robust baby—there was nothing limp or delicate about him. When he cried he pounded his fists and kicked his sturdy legs in unison with a low-pitched wail that could be heard two blocks away. Thankfully, he was easily satisfied. He drank in great, desperate gulps, and he finished his meal in ten minutes flat. Then he was all coos and charms until the next mealtime, when he changed into a miniature tyrant again. Mr. and Mrs. Foxworthy were charmed with baby Gus, and loved him as one of their own. But I could tell it was exhausting for them, as much as they tried not to show it. I did my best to tend to the baby and keep him content, but he had a set of lungs on him to rival an ambulance siren, and his hunger hit him instantly, followed by the already described wail set at full volume from the first cry.

One evening when the baby had been especially trying, I came out into the living room after at last soothing him to sleep. At two and a half months old, he already seemed to have a mind of his own about these things. I sat down on the couch and my whole body felt numb. I hardly had the energy to move my mouth to speak a word, but I felt like something needed to be said. I felt overwhelmed with guilt for crashing into the Foxworthy's lives the way I had, and causing so much trouble for them. So I said, "I just want to say I'm sorry. You both have been so good to me. I don't want to be a burden to you, and I know that I am. It's not right for you to have to hear the baby crying all the time, and have no peace in your home. So as soon as I can I'll take the baby, and I'll find someplace else to live."

Mrs. Foxworthy put down her work, looked over at Jake, and the two of them exchanged a look. Sometimes married people do that—they just look at each other, and a whole conversation can happen without one word spoken aloud. Jake gave a little nod, then folded his newspaper and put it on the end table. Mrs. Foxworthy said, "Well, now, Jake and I have just been talking about these things. As much as we care about you and little Gus, I think all four of us together in this little trailer is a bit much for everyone, and a few of the neighbors have complained. They're all retired you see, so of course they're not used to a little one that gets hungry in the night. But we think we've come up with an idea of something we can do for you. We haven't ironed out all the details yet, but so far it looks like it might work."

I sat there still, waiting. Too tired to feel or respond to anything.

"You know Jake's mother of course, who lives across the river in Houghten. She's in her early 90's, and she still lives on her own. In the past we talked about having her come live with us, but she doesn't want to. She has her home, and her friends close by and her pinochle club, and she can't drive around like she used to, so she wants to stay put. Well I can't say I blame her—I'm sure that's what we'd all want at her age. But she's getting so she needs someone there. And she has that big house to take care of, with several extra rooms. So Jake and I had the idea, what if we moved in with her? Now that we're going to church across the river and Jake no longer works in town, there's really no reason for us to live here instead of there, and it's even better and more convenient to live over there, really. We can visit our friends in town anytime, it's only a 15 minute drive. We've talked it over with Jake's mother, and as much as she hates to admit needing any help, she was thrilled with the idea of staying in her own home."

"Then you, Flora, could stay in this place. The trailer is paid for, so there's no worry about that. As for the neighbors—that's the part we need to look into. Jake has a little piece of property on the edge of town out by the high school that belonged to his father. It's just a dusty old lot, really—it's not much to look at. We've never quite known what to do with it. The ice house used to be there, it's quite shady and cool in the summer. Anyhow, what we've been thinking is, what if we had this trailer moved onto that lot for you? We still need to check about the water and the electrical hook ups, but you certainly wouldn't have any close neighbors to worry about. The trailer is in a retirement community now, so it couldn't stay here. Of course, this is all just an idea. We were going to wait until we had worked things out more before we told you about it. But we've talked it through with Jake's mother and the boys already, and they all think it's a good idea, so really there's no reason not to go ahead and tell you now. And I do think in the end we can make it work."

I stared from one to the other of them, afraid of some gross misunderstanding. Maybe I'd fallen asleep somehow while I was sitting there, and I'd heard things all wrong. I simply couldn't believe it. But they just kept looking at me, waiting for a response, so at last I had to say something.

"You mean . . . you mean, you'd just move out, and give me your *home*?" I said at last.

"Well, yes," said Mrs. Foxworthy. "I suppose that's what we mean." She looked at Jake, and he nodded. "But we won't need it, and the boys both told us they don't need it or want it. We would have a nice home ourselves, nicer than this one in fact. That old house is far too big for Jake's mother, and it will be his of course when she's gone, he's an only child. We would just be moving sooner rather than later, with no harm to anyone as far as we can see, and quite a bit of benefit to everyone all around."

"But I can't pay you for it," I said.

"Oh, Child," said Mrs. Foxworthy, "Certainly you don't think we would ask you to pay for it! The trailer would stay in our name until you're a bit older. You can think of yourself as a caretaker if you like. But once you're old enough, we would like to give it to you. There are ladies in town who have things you can do to pay for your electricity and phone and water bills, I've been asking around a little, I hope you don't mind. Really, you can think of it as doing us a favor. I hate the thought of selling this place to just any person on the street. It isn't worth much money, but it has been our home. I even asked the Lord once why he would give us two homes when we only needed one. I suppose now I have my answer! He knew you and little Gus were going to need a place to live, and I do think that with you being so young, you would have a hard time finding a good situation. Well, He always knows, doesn't he? I'm just happy things can work out so nicely. And if that isn't just like the Lord, I don't know what is!"

Mrs. Foxworthy had stopped, breathless and flushed, and

looked over at her husband again. Mr. Foxworthy looked at me and gave another nod. Then he leaned forward in his chair, and said, "Now, don't you think of this as charity, Flora. We want to see you and little Gus provided for. We've come to think of you as one of our own children."

I looked from one to the other of them. They both looked happy and sincere. And it was all just too much for me to believe. I felt too shocked to respond, to say yes, or even to say thank you. I'd never known there were people like this in the world, people who were kind and good all the way through, with no hidden motives to be suspicious of, nothing to be wary of, and nothing to hold my guard up against.

As they sat there looking at me their faces began to change, from happy excitement to worry and concern, and I knew I had to say something. So finally I said, "Well, I guess I just need to think about it for a while. It's all just too much. Maybe after I go to sleep and then wake up, I can try to believe it."

Jake chuckled and picked up his paper again. Mrs. Foxworthy laughed, and said, "Yes, sleep is the best thing for you. You're all worn out, and here we are springing such a big idea on you late at night, and little Gus will be waking up and crying for his breakfast before you know it. For goodness sake, it's past eleven o'clock. Past time for us all to be in bed!"

I got up and started down the hall, but then I stopped and turned around, and said, "You all have been so good to me. And I know I don't deserve any of it."

"Oh, but none of us do. That's the whole point, you see," Mrs. Foxworthy said. Jake looked over his paper and nodded again. This statement apparently made perfectly clear sense to both of them. It didn't make much sense to me, but I just nodded and said good night, and walked the rest of the way to my room. Even though I was so tired, I sat up for a long time thinking, listening to baby Gus snoring softly an arm's length away in his borrowed bassinet. It seemed like ever since I'd come to this place, there'd been wave after wave of goodness. First it came and washed over my feet, then it was up past my knees, then my waist. In the end it swept me off my feet entirely, each wave bigger and more powerful than the last, until I no longer had any sure footing left at all. High time I learn to swim, I chuckled to myself. Float along in that current, and swim in the grace of God.

I'd always believed that if I tried my best to live in the right way, God would help me out, and somehow or another, I would make it. But I thought life would be hard, and that I'd have to make it on my own. I hadn't expected to be surrounded by love and help, and have people—white people no less—help me out like this. The Foxworthys had been so good to me. And they never made me feel like I owed them anything. In fact, they made me feel like I was the one doing them a favor to let them help me out. That night, my heart felt full to bursting. I felt more grateful to them than I could ever say.

More than just taking pity on me, they seemed to actually like having me around. They made me feel like I was a part of their own family. Mr. Foxworthy had said I was like a daughter to him. Now, that was something to think about! I wondered what their boys would think of that. I'd met both of them over the Christmas holidays, and they'd looked me up and down with frank curiosity, though not unfriendliness. They took their parents' love and affection for granted, and didn't pay me much mind. As much as possible I'd tried to stay in the background and let the family have their time together. Other than holidays, both sons seemed to be busy with their own lives. I think Mr. and Mrs. Foxworthy missed them something terrible, though they didn't talk about it. I'm sure they would have liked their sons to live nearer by, and to come more often. They would have loved some grandchildren too.

Mr. Foxworthy was so different than my other Daddy, than my brothers and their friends and the kind of men I'd known back home. I shuddered when I thought of them, then I quickly shut the door on those memories. I didn't want thoughts like that coming in to invade my peaceful little room. I was in a new place now. A good place. The old things had passed away.

I turned all that thinking over in my mind as I lay awake to catch the baby as soon as he cried. Even if I couldn't give the Foxworthys much in return for all they'd done for me, for that night at least, I could give them a good night's sleep.

Part Two: Paul

CHAPTER TWELVE

Saturday morning, visiting day. Mrs. Sarah Pinehurst, wife of the Reverend Steven Pinehurst, stood on the tiny wooden porch in a navy polyester crepe dress with a slim matching belt, pleated skirt, and a high-necked ruffled collar. In one hand she held a large purse filled with tracts and invitations to Sunday services at the First Baptist Church of Spring, Idaho. In the other she firmly grasped the hand of a squirming two year old boy, dressed in stiff twill pants and a button down shirt, tugging furiously at her hand and fussing to play. Behind her stood another boy, age 8, awkward and knobbly and thin, cowering behind his mother's skirt and praying to God that no one from his class at school would be behind the door. That boy was me.

Every Saturday was visiting day. Father needed silence, Mother said, to work on his sermon, so we went visiting. Sometimes we went to see the old people. Mom would sit and listen to them talk on and on about their aches and pains, or sometimes they would talk about their lost husbands and grown children. If they were really old, they would talk about when *they* were children—the same few stories, over and over again. Those visits were long and dull, but endurable. Other mornings, we would visit the heathen—people who didn't go to church on Sundays, or Catholics. Mother would rap on the door and invite herself in. Then there we'd be, in somebody else's living room. Sometimes people would listen politely, but other times they made no pretense about the fact that they just wanted us to go away. The worst was when they had kids my age. The kids would peer around the corner of the wall at us, giggling and whispering. I could see the malicious spark in their eyes, and knew that come Monday, I would be the butt of their jokes again—the Preacher's kid.

Mother didn't let us play with the heathen. Instead, we were made to sit quietly with our hands folded in our laps while she shared the gospel with them, or tried to at least. My brother Jeremy rarely sat quietly, and Mother had a hard time managing him. She shifted him from arm to arm, stopping every few minutes to scold him, while trying to include all four points of the gospel at the same time. It made a pretty comical scene sometimes, though I dared not laugh. If Mother got really upset with us, she would tell Father when we got home. And that was a scenario I had learned if at all possible to avoid.

So there we stood on the porch of a small turquoise and white aluminum trailer, on the far edge of town out past the high school. I'd rarely been in this part of town. Maybe Mom had worn out her welcome in the usual neighborhoods, and had driven around looking for new places to go. There weren't any other houses around. The paved road ended in the parking lot in front of the high school, where she had left the car. It was fall, and overcast and gray, but still warm. I could hear the wind whistling through the trees behind the little trailer. Pine needles were scattered across the bare dirt yard in front, but the porch was swept clean.

My Mother's rap-rap-rap sounded on the thin door, and then it opened to reveal a black woman, tall and thin, wearing a plain dress with no stockings and a scarf tied over her hair. Neither Jeremy nor I had ever seen a black person up close before, so I imagine we gaped and stared with eyes as wide as china plates. "Yes?" the woman asked, in her rich, black voice. Mother seemed very surprised, and said all a-fluster, "I didn't realize this was your house ... I'm so sorry."

"Won't you come in?" the woman said, and stepped aside to let us pass. Mother hesitated for a few seconds, then made up her mind and stepped through. We found ourselves in a small L-shaped room, plain but tidy, with worn brown carpet and wood paneling on the walls. A green couch stood against the wall facing the front window, a big rocking chair sat next to the black wood stove, and a rectangular table with three chairs around it was pushed against the wall by the kitchen. A sliding glass door led out to the backyard and the woods behind. A big picture of Jesus praying hung on the wall above the table, and in it Jesus was holding a necklace of beads and looked all glowing.

"Let me take your coats, and get you some tea," the woman

said, and then added, "Run along now boys, and play with my son Gus—he's down the hall in his bedroom." And believe you me, I took little Jeremy's hand and we ran, before Mother could say or do anything to stop us. As we started down the dim, narrow hall, a shadow suddenly sprang out at us with a huge ROAR. I startled visibly and yelled out, and Jeremy was so scared he grabbed me around the waist, practically pulling me down, and then he got the hiccups. And that's when I got my first look at Gus Kenover, with his chocolate-milk brown skin, green eyes, and pale kinky hair, doubled over laughing in the hall. Swift steps sounded from behind and Gus's Mama stood, with her hands on her hips, frowning down at him. "Now Gus," she said, "Is that any way to treat our guests?"

Immediately Gus stood up straight and said, "No, Mama," and looked her in the eye with genuine contriteness. Later on I would learn that Gus could stand a lot of things, but disappointing his Mama wasn't one of them.

"Now then," the lady said, her voice firm. "Why don't you take these boys into your room and play. And I don't want any fuss about sharin'. Toys are for sharin'. All right?"

"All right," Gus said, and we followed him to his room at the end of the hall. The room was plain and mostly bare. There was a twin bed, neatly made up with one of those quilts that have squares in every color of the rainbow, the kind usually made out of old clothes. Over the bed there was a picture of a white-winged angel leading a little girl and boy over a rickety bridge, with water crashing underneath. It was the only picture in the room, which is probably why I remember it. A mangy stuffed dog lay on the bed, propped up against a pillow. "That's Rudy," said Gus, pointing at the toy. "Mama says I can't have a real dog, so I have him instead."

On one side of the room there was a painted bookshelf, the cheap press board kind, where you fit the slots together like a puzzle. On the shelves there were a few books and several shoe boxes. Inside each box was a different kind of toy. There were blocks in one, and green plastic army men in another. One held a cowboy hat and holsters with toy guns, and another had matchbox-sized trucks and cars. A box that held magazine clippings, photographs and greeting cards was lying half emptied on the floor. Gus held up a worn picture. "This is what I'm going to ask Santa for next Christmas," he said. It was a picture of a train set. "It has an engine that blows real steam, and coal cars, and freight cars, and an engineer and a real caboose and everything."

"Cool," I said, crouching down on the floor to look at the picture with him. Then, seeing Jeremy heading for the box, I added, "You'd better put these away. My brother might rip them up."

Gus stuffed all the pictures back in the box and put it up on the highest shelf, then got down the box with the cowboy stuff and pistols. "Let's play cowboys," he said. "I'll be the Lone Ranger, you be Tonto, and your brother can be the horse thief we capture."

"Okay," I said, and we started to play. Before long, I heard the quick, indignant steps of my mother coming down the hall. She stood in the doorway, frowning, disapproving, and unsure. "Paul," my mother said nervously. "You know your father disapproves of this wild sort of play."

"Aw Mom," I said, ready to reel out protests, desperate to capture another moment of real fun. Then from behind my mother, the smooth voice of Mrs. Kenover called out, "Boys, come to the table now. It's time for your cocoa."

"Oh yeah—cocoa!" Gus shouted, dropping his holster and hat.

"Yeah—cocoa!" I yelled too, dropping my pistol and following Gus right past my mother, with Jeremy toddling after us shouting something in his two year old garble. When we got to the table there were three mugs of hot chocolate, big ones for Gus and me, and a little plastic one for Jeremy. There was also a plate with saltine crackers on it, a knife alongside a tub of margarine, and a jar of honey. We dug in with zeal.

"You know boys, how they play. So wild," my mother said nervously, following us into the room.

Mrs. Kenover looked at her in reply but said nothing, and finished pouring tea for her and Mom. Then she sat down in her rocking chair, looked out the window reflectively, and said, "God has given you two beautiful boys—beautiful boys. I reckon my Gus and your Paul are about the same age, if memory serves me right. Now," she said, looking directly at my Mom, "Tell me why you've come."

Mother was taken aback, and for once she had nothing to say. She stammered something about a neighborly call.

"Just a friendly call, uhmm hmmm. No, I reckon you think I've gone over to the heathen, and want me to come back to the Baptists, is that it? Or maybe you just came out of curiosity."

Mother just sat there quiet, struck dumb by such a direct question.

"Well, I'm not going back to the Baptists, so you can save your time over me. The Catholics have been right good to me, in my times of need. And Lord knows I've had plenty of them. Father Johnston is a kind man, and even when folks are disapprovin' of him, he's the same. So if we have a few differences of opinion over things like how to pray, or the communion bread, or things of that kind, it's of no account to me. He has the love of Jesus in him," Mrs. Kenover said, looking squarely at Mother. "And that's what counts, isn't it?"

Mother said she wasn't sure about that, but said maybe they could talk about it more some other time.

"Anytime," Mrs. Kenover said in her rich smooth voice. "You're welcome here anytime. I've enjoyed seeing your boys, and I dare say Gus has enjoyed it too. His school friends mostly live across the river, and we don't have a car. It's good for him to have a friend over to play. So you come on over anytime."

We visited the Kenovers on many Saturdays after that. I was glad, because at Mrs. Kenover's house I got to play, and Mama didn't say one word about it. Maybe because she was afraid of offending

Mrs. Kenover, or maybe because Mrs. Kenover just didn't allow it. Gus never teased me about being a preacher's kid, probably because he was different too. Besides, he went to the Catholic school across the river in Houghten. A special van, driven by Mr. Foxworthy, came to pick up him and a few other kids on school mornings. We never went to the same school until high school.

Everyone called Mrs. Kenover Missus, even though she wasn't married. She was more like a respectable, fine lady than any other mother I knew, and it seemed out of place to call her by her first name, or by a young name like Miss. She couldn't have been very old, but she always seemed sort of ageless to me. Maybe because of her different appearance, or her steady, calm personality. She didn't nag or scold like most mothers, and she stood tall and stately, even though she never had any fancy clothes.

During our visits Mrs. Kenover usually sat quietly, working on some mending or knitting while my Mother talked on about the differences between Catholics and Protestants, or what the word of God said on this subject or on that. Sometimes if we played in the living room, I would catch Mrs. Kenover looking over at my Mom out of the corner of her eye, watching her keenly, sizing her up. But only when Mother wasn't looking.

After a time my Mother would stop talking, rest the back of her head against the sofa, look out the window at the trees and just be quiet for a while. Then Mrs. Kenover would rise up quietly to fill her cup with more tea, which Mom would drink in silence. Mrs. Kenover would smile a little into her knitting, and it was like she was taking care of my Mother, watching over her, nurturing the quiet which seemed to let all the muscles in my Mom's face fall slack a little, which seemed to allow her to sigh and breathe a little more deep. Mom would get a sad, wistful expression on her face then. But before much time had passed she would come to, apologize for forgetting herself, and hustle Jeremy and me off to finish our visiting. And the peace which minutes before had seemed to settle over her whole body would vanish, like a puff of warm breath in the chilly Spring air.

CHAPTER THIRTEEN

"My dad's an army pilot. A commander," Gus bragged, one Saturday while we were setting up army men in his room.

"Oh yeah? Where does he fly?"

"He's a long, long way from here on a secret assignment. Probably India, or Africa, or someplace like that."

"He is not," I said. "I don't believe you."

"Yeah, well, he could be. Mama says she doesn't know where my dad is. She never knew him too well, and they were never married. So I figure he could be an army pilot in Africa, and way too busy on secret assignments to contact us. But he will someday, I bet."

"I bet he's not. I bet he's just an old bum."

Gus shoved me hard, pinning me against the floor. The leg of his bed pressed hard against my right shoulder, and the army men scattered all around.

"Ouch!" I said, "You're hurting me!"

"You take that back, Paul Pinehurst," he yelled, his fist held up ready to pummel my face.

"OK, OK, I will," I said, shoving his hands off of me and sitting up. Gus's temper was like that—it flared up instantly from a tiny spark to a full blaze, like spontaneous combustion. "But still," I said, unwilling to surrender my point completely, "I bet he isn't no army pilot in Africa."

"Let's set up the train," I said. Gus pushed the army men to the side in a pile, and got down the box. For a while, we were quiet, setting up the new track and trains Gus had gotten for Christmas. It was the same as the one in the picture he had shown me the day we first met, with a shiny black engine that ran on an electric track, blew real steam and whistled. Jeremy was sitting up on the bed, smashing two toy trucks together, over and over again. Gus had given him the trucks so he wouldn't smash the train cars. Smashing things was Jeremy's favorite way to play.

"We pray for my dad every night," Gus said.

"What do you pray?" I asked.

"We pray that he'll repent of his wicked ways, turn to Jesus, and be restored to the fellowship of Christ and the saints."

"What does that mean?" I said.

"I don't know. That's just what Mama prays. I agree and say

amen. I think she still loves him."

"I thought you said they were never married."

"They weren't. I think he hurt her real bad, and she says she was just a girl, not even a woman yet. But she still loves him. Anyway, my Mama says we should pray for him every day, seeing as he's my blood father. Mr. Foxworthy, he's my real dad. Or maybe my Grandpa, he's pretty old. Do you know what?" Gus asked in a low voice, solemn and important. "It was Mr. Foxworthy that bought me the train set, not Santa Claus. I heard Mama thanking him for it after Christmas dinner."

"Really?"

"Really," Gus said importantly. "Santa Claus is all just a big trick, so grown-ups can get you stuff in secret."

"I already knew he wasn't real," I said.

"You did?" Gus's face fell.

"My Mom told me ages ago that Santa wasn't real. At our house, we aren't allowed to talk about Santa, because that's heathen."

"You're not allowed to talk about Santa?" Gus asked, unbelievingly.

"Nope. Christmas should be about worshiping God. Santa is of the world, and what the heathen people celebrate instead of the birth of Jesus."

"Do you still get presents?" Gus asked.

"Of course we still get presents. We just don't talk about Santa."

"Oh," Gus said. "I guess that's OK then, if you still get presents. Otherwise it would stink."

Just when we had finished setting up the track and Gus was carefully putting on the engine and all the cars, Jeremy came down from the bed and kicked the track, messing it all up. "Mom!" I yelled, diving for Jeremy and then pinning him down, away from the trains. "Jeremy's messing up our track!"

Mother came down the hall to fetch Jeremy and drag him away, kicking and screaming. I closed the door behind them. "You're lucky you don't have a brother," I said to Gus. "He always messes everything up."

"Maybe," said Gus. "I dunno. I always thought it would be fun to have a whole bunch of brothers and sisters, like eight or ten of them. Then there'd always be someone to play with."

"You can have Jeremy any time you want," I said. "All he does is break my things, and get me in trouble. I wish he was never born."

"You shouldn't say that, about your own brother," Gus said, looking up at me seriously.

"Yeah, well, what do you know about anything?" I said. Gus's house was always peaceful and quiet. He didn't even know what fights were. Suddenly I hated him, and I felt so angry I threw a piece of track right at his face, missing him by a few inches. I never did have good aim.

"Maybe I know more about some things than you, Mr. Smarty Pants," Gus said back, standing up, ready to fight. And then my Mom called for me, and it was time to go.

I walked out of the Kenover's trailer that Saturday feeling sick to my stomach, the angry words left hanging, heavy and unresolved, in the air. In the car driving home, the familiar feeling of dread, the fear of what would happen next, dropped over me like a thick, smothering blanket. I started to cry, a baby thing to do for a ten year old. Mom asked me what was wrong, but I turned my face and pressed it against the cold car window.

I'd never had a real friend before. I was the Preacher's kid, the one everyone else teased and tormented, the one who hid in the bathroom during recess. And now just when things were finally going good, everything was spoiled, and it was all my fault. That was the first real fight Gus and I ever had. But a couple of Saturdays later when we went to visit again, Gus had forgotten all about it, and we played just like before. Gus was always quick to get angry, but even quicker to forget and forgive. And though I didn't know it back then, he was the last guy in the world to ditch a friend.

CHAPTER FOURTEEN

By the time I was in fifth grade, we visited the Kenover's trailer almost every Saturday. Instead of the worst day of the week, Saturday had become the high point of my life. I don't think Mom genuinely needed to go there for her visiting, but she usually found some excuse. Probably it was the high point of her week, too.

Gus went to the Catholic school across the river in Houghten. I went to Lincoln Primary, Spring's public grade school. It didn't take long for the other kids to learn that my best friend was the son of the only black person in town. Then they tormented me about that, too. A few times I had gotten into fights over it, but I wasn't much of a fighter. But Gus never cared that I was different, or teased me about my dad. With his kinky hair, green eyes, and light brown skin, he was different, too.

If Gus paid attention to people's comments, he sure never showed it. Maybe because Gus just naturally loved everybody, and after being around him for five minutes, most people loved Gus. He had a way of winning people over that I could never figure out. Maybe he didn't hear much teasing anyway. He and his Mama pretty much kept to themselves. Mrs. Kenover didn't have a car and had her groceries delivered, and she rarely came into town for errands. For the most part, she had the respect of the town people—you never heard a mean comment about her. But she never had any real friends that I could see. Except for of course the Foxworthys.

One Saturday when I was about 12, just after the Christmas holidays, we knocked on the trailer door. As we came in, shedding coats and scarves and gloves, there was a different feel in the house. Mrs. Kenover was polite as always, but her face looked tight and worried, and the house was cold.

"I'm sorry, I'm out of tea," she apologized. "Would you like a glass of water?"

"Goodness gracious!" said Mother, "Don't you have any heat?"

Mrs. Kenover looked her in the eye and said, "No, Mrs. Pinehurst, we do not. I have been sick and fell behind in my work, and I was not able to pay my bill."

"Aren't your Catholics taking care of you?" Mother said, smugness in her voice.

Mrs. Kenover stiffened. "Father Tim has been away for some time, taking care of his dying mother."

"Hmmm," said Mother absently. "Just like a Catholic."

"Mrs. Pinehurst, if you would like to help in some practical way, you are welcome to stay. But if you are here to insult those who have been kind to me, you are not welcome."

Mother, in shock and consternation, huffed, and then elaborately, slowly, began gathering our things. "If you felt that way about it," she said, "You might have told me before. I'll just . . . be going now . . . .", she said, buttoning her last button. Her voice was high pitched and quavering. "Come along now boys. We're not wanted here."

Gus and I watched our mothers from opposite sides of the room as if we were watching a tennis match, our eyes bobbing from one woman to the other. Jeremy started pitching a fit, screaming, "Cowboy guns! Cowboy guns!" and punched and kicked at my mother as she struggled to get his rubber boots back on. Mrs. Kenover watched her with a weary expression and held the door open, standing to the side so we could exit, which at long last we did. "I'll see you later, Paul," Gus called after us. I turned and said, "Yeah, see you later," and followed my Mom's back out to the car.

It took forever for Mom to get the still kicking and screaming Jeremy strapped in to the backseat. Then she drove down a couple of streets, pulled over to the side of the road, and turned and said to me, "The nerve of that woman! Can you believe what she just said to me? Can you believe it?" Then she burst into tears. She pulled back out onto the street, and dabbed at her eyes with a tissue all the rest of the way home.

I suppose Mrs. Kenover had simply had her fill of Mom's railing against Catholics, and of all her religious talk. She was sick and worn out and she simply had too much work to do. When she closed the door on us that day I heard her mutter something about the Pharisees and their religion, and something about the book of James.

So that was the end of our Saturday visits to Mrs. Kenover's trailer, for a while anyway. Eventually my Mom found her way back in to Gus's Mama's good graces, but for the time being, Saturdays became once again a dull and hated ritual, and I sorely missed the hot cocoa and saltine crackers beneath the big glowing picture of Jesus at that kitchen table. And I missed the way Mother would relax sometimes, with her head resting against the back of the sofa, and the soft click-clicking sound of Mrs. Kenover's knitting needles, and of course playing with Gus. But it didn't matter nearly so much as it might have, because by that time I was old enough to ride my bike over and visit after school whenever I wanted, which I did more and more as time went on. The overall peacefulness and firm affection I found inside that little trailer was an escape from the awful tensity, the shrill nagging, and the cold silences of my own house.

When you walked in my front door, the air felt taut and loaded, like a rubber band pulled too tight and ready to snap. When I came home from school, Mom would be sitting on the couch, staring into space. I would try to creep past her and head straight up to my room, but almost always she called out, "Paul, come greet your Mother." So I would go, give her a kiss on the cheek, and mumble through the answers when she asked me about my day. I knew that almost anything I said would make her upset and she would give me a lecture, so I tried to say as little as possible. Then I would go to my room, change out of my school clothes, and leave as soon as I could for Gus's house. If he wasn't home, I'd go to the schoolyard and shoot baskets. Mom would watch me head off from the big picture window in our living room, biting her lip and frowning, but saying nothing.

Six o'clock or so I'd come home, and there she'd be, banging around in the kitchen. The more upset she was, the louder she banged, so I stayed in my room and did homework until I was called down to the table. When Father came home, the rubber band was pulled even tighter. Throughout dinner, he always looked displeased. He shot demanding questions from one to the other of us, and we just tried to think of whatever answers would upset him the least. Before dinner was over, more often than not there was some kind of argument. When he wasn't the one talking Father was quiet and cold, and my Mom just got shriller and more emotional the longer it went on. Jeremy and I slipped out to the family room as soon as we could, where we'd watch TV, mess around, or get into a fight.

On good nights, Father had a meeting. Elders' meetings, Deacons' meetings, Sunday School Teacher meetings, Building Committee meetings—he went to them all. On nights when he didn't have a meeting, he would retreat to his study to work on whatever it is that pastors work on in there, for hours and hours. I never thought about how Mom felt on those nights, always left alone. The arguments left hanging in the cold air like icicles hanging off the edge of a roof, ready to fall and shatter and stab. Around eight thirty she'd come and shuffle Jeremy to his bath and bed. When I went up at nine, sometimes she would come and perch on the end of my bed, just sitting there and saying nothing for a long time. Once in a blue moon I could get her to tell a story of sing a hymn. She had a beautiful voice for singing, quiet and soft and sweet. She would never sing in public, Father gave up asking long ago. But sometimes, just when it was Jeremy or I, she would sing. Then I'd close my eyes and wish she could be like that all the time. That life could be like that all the time. Peaceful and calm, the way it was when she was singing.

CHAPTER FIFTEEN

Sometimes when I visited their trailer, Gus's Mama would tell us stories of when she was growing up. Of course everyone in town was dying to know where she came from, how she came out here, and all the details of how she got Gus. But they never had a chance to find out. She wasn't the sort of person you could push to reveal what she didn't want you to know. But a few times after school Gus and I got her to tell us stories about when she was young, and the things she told us gave me a look into another side of the world I would never have known about, if I hadn't known her.

"How I loved to read, when I was a girl," she said once, as she sat in the wooden rocking chair by the wood stove, her knitting or mending in her lap. "I didn't always get to go to school, and sometimes even when I did, there wasn't much learning to be had. We lived in a bad neighborhood. But somehow or other I learned to read. I would sneak out of the house early on Saturday mornings, walk to the library, and wait for them to open their doors. The librarian there was kind to me, as so few were in those days, and she would give me books to read. I lapped them up one after the other, like an alley cat that hadn't had a scrap of food for days. Sometimes I would go to the big dictionary on the stand and look up the words I didn't know. Then I would write those words down on a list and practice them—practice, practice. My Daddy and uncles teased me something terrible for puttin' on airs, but I didn't care. This was my ticket to another world, and I thought, I'm going to be part of that world someday. And here I am, little Flora Suzette, living in a home of my own in a nice little town and raising you up, Gus. How my Momma would love to see me now!"

"I tried for a while to teach Momma to read, but Daddy didn't like it, and he would beat her if he found out. He said Momma had no need for readin', that it would only ruin her for her true duties as a wife. Maybe he was right, in a way. My Momma had a hard life. There was always a load of work to do. She wouldn't have had any time to read even if she did learn how. She was a quiet woman, a long-suffering woman. She just bore things, and she never complained. But she prayed. Daddy could stop her from doing a lot of things, but he couldn't stop her from that. I just wish she could see me now."

"Why doesn't she come visit?" I asked.

"Oh, goodness Lord," Mrs. Kenover chuckled. "If only it were that easy! Momma would never make it out all this way. I told you she can barely read or write, and she's never been twenty miles outside the neighborhood where she's lived her whole life. A trip like that would right scare her into the grave. And Lord knows I'm never going back there. I don't even know whether she's dead now, or still living. Sometimes I imagine she's up there already, sittin' right in the crook of the arm of Jesus, looking down and seeing me here and smiling. If she isn't there in body, she's up there in spirit for sure. It would make her smile to see us three sitting here. So I imagine the Lord lets her see a little one way or another, so she can know all her hoping and praying paid off in the end, despite all."

Times we could get her to talk, we loved sitting and listening to Gus's Mama. But those times were few and brief. After twenty minutes or so which we did our best not to interrupt, she would come to herself and say, "Look at me here, my ironing in a pile and the wrinkles setting it! Lazy as a fat old spoiled cat. You boys run along now, and play. I have to get back to work now."

Mrs. Kenover worked hard, taking in washing and ironing and doing sewing and for other people so she could earn the money she and Gus needed to live. I wondered if she still liked novels, or ever had time to read anymore. I never saw any books around, except for the thick, worn Bible with its cracked leather cover. She read that enough for sure.

CHAPTER SIXTEEN

When scolding Gus, Mrs. Kenover would sometimes call him by his full name—Augustine Francis Kenover.

"Where'd you get such a weird name?" I asked once, as we walked down the dirt trail, following the river. It was the summer we were both 12, just before Junior High.

"Don't ever call me that!" Gus said vehemently, fists clenched to show me he meant it.

"All right, all right, I won't. But I still want to know how you got it. It sounds like a girl's name."

Gus scowled. "It's the name of some saint—some holy man who lived ages and ages ago. My middle name was also my dad's name, but my Mom says that isn't why she used it. She says my dad was no good, but I'm supposed to redeem the name.

"What's that supposed to mean?" I said.

"I dunno. I've heard the word in church before, but I never knew what it meant."

"Me neither. I could ask my Dad someday. He knows stuff like that."

"Yeah, and when you find out, don't tell him why you're asking."

"Huh?"

"My name, Stupid. Don't tell him my full name, or anyone, ever. You have to swear."

"Okay."

"You swear it?" he said.

"Hereby, I solemnly swear, I will never utter the name Augustine Francis Kenover, to anyone. Except I just did."

"Good," he smiled. "Then I won't call you a P.K."

"What's a P.K.?" I asked innocently.

"Preacher's Kid!" he yelled, and then I punched him, and then we were on the ground, wrestling and grunting until we had rolled almost to the edge of the river, clutching our stomachs from laughing so hard.

On a Sunday morning during that same summer, Gus went to church with me. There was a visiting preacher that day, a traveling evangelist from another district. He was a giant, silver haired man with a thundering voice, and as he proclaimed the gospel from the book of Romans, the room got quieter and quieter, until all you could hear were the great volcanic booms of his voice, with the noiseless sound of people holding their breath in between. At the end of the sermon he gave an altar call. No sooner had he said the words then Gus stood up.

"What are you doing?" I whispered fiercely.

"I'm going up there. I've got to go up."

"You can't do that!" I said, but he was already going. There we were, right in the front where the Pastor's family sat, and Gus stood up and walked down. He took his place in front of the pulpit in a line with several others, while the Evangelist prayed blessings over all our new brothers and sisters in the faith, and gave thanks to heaven for the salvation of their souls.

After church was over we walked to Gus's place, taking the long way along the river. When we had walked in silence for awhile, Gus said suddenly, "I never knew that before."

"Never knew what," I said.

"That I could be washed clean from all my sins. Man, I've sinned tons of times. Sometimes Mama takes me to the church on Fridays and I confess. But I never knew I could be washed clean."

"Yeah, well, you can. I've heard that hundreds of times."

"Well, goody for you," Gus said. He wasn't in the mood to

fight. His face was all lit up like a Christmas tree, and he was smiling. "Last one to the steps is a big fat girl!" he said, and took off like a jet. I took off after him, my heart slamming hard into my chest as I strained to catch up. Usually I was the faster runner, but that day he was unbeatable.

When we got to the little trailer he went inside and immediately told his Mama what he'd done, how he'd gone up to the front and gotten cleansed from all his sins. At first Mrs. Kenover just stood there, not speaking. I thought she was mad, and that she was going to let him have it for going up and looking bad in front of all the town people. But instead she seized him up in a great big hug. "Well, I'm right proud of you, Gus! I'm right proud!" she said.

When she let him go at last, she said, "Now, you boys run along, and I'm going to bake us all a cake—a chocolate cake, with whip cream frosting. This is a day to celebrate."

"Come on!" said Gus, and we headed out the back door to work on the army base we were building behind his house. Mr. Foxworthy had brought over piles of old wood, rope, barrels, discarded tires, and other assorted junk, and he was letting us borrow all the tools and nails we needed to build it. Once in a while he would stop by to check on our progress and give advice. I still remember that summer as the summer of the fort, and think back on all the hours we spent building it and playing in it—even sleeping all night high up on the platform we had built between the two tallest trees. Back then it was still just Gus and me—it was before we went to High School and Gus became the big man on campus, and before

Gus discovered girls. I remember as we worked that day, in between the sounds of pounding nails and sawing wood I could hear the clatter of pans and bowls and spoons, and Mrs. Kenover singing hymns in her rich, deep voice, the music wafting through the mesh of the sliding door she'd left open to catch the breeze.

And all through that afternoon, through the celebration lunch and cake and everything, I felt rotten and hollow inside. For once, I was the left-out one. I'd been told these things all my life, and nobody had ever celebrated over me. I'd known about these things since I was old enough to breath, and I didn't see what there was to make any fuss about.

Afterward, Gus was different, a little. At least when he did something bad or mean, he seemed to feel sorry for it afterward, and would even go up to the person and apologize. "Come on," I would say, "this is stupid." But he'd say no, he had to do it. And sometimes when I was there, I heard him and his Mama pray together, and they prayed like nothing I had ever heard before. It was like they were really talking to somebody, and just talking regular. But most of the time he was the same old Gus, full of crazy ideas and fun, and we didn't talk about religion much. I got enough of that at my house to have my fill for a lifetime.

Part Three: Gus

CHAPTER SEVENTEEN

I was fourteen years old, the summer I grew from a boy to a man. I can even tell you the date—July 21st, 1984. I remember it was a muggy night, hot and still. Even the crickets that always seemed to make a racket around nightfall were quiet.

Mama had read in the paper about the rallies north of Coeur d'Alene in Hayden at the Aryan Nations compound. But we never thought in our little town it would have anything to do with us. People rarely came to Spring unless they came on purpose. There was a gas station and a hotel with a restaurant attached right off the highway, but there wasn't any reason for most people to drive further on in to town. We'd heard that a few locals were sympathetic with Richard Butler, the leader of the Aryan Nations white supremacist group, and his type—some of the radicals who lived outside town and off the grid. The state of Idaho seems to attract people like that, refugees from society for one reason or another. But mostly they kept to themselves. If you left them alone and didn't pry, they were generally did the same for you.

Anyway, we were sitting in the living room that night, Mama with some kind of work and me with a hot rod magazine, when we heard a couple of motorbikes pull in to the front yard, loud as jackhammers. Their headlights blared in through the drapes pulled across our front window. Mama looked at me and I looked back, and neither one of us said one word or made a move. We just waited to see what would happen next.

Pretty soon we could hear them out there shuffling their feet in the dirt, laughing and swearing. Then they started throwing rocks at the trailer. I got up, ignoring Mama's sharp whisper telling me to keep still, and peeked through the side of the window. I saw three of them, one old guy in a t-shirt and vest with a long gray beard, a bandanna around his head, and a huge gut hanging out over his pants, and two younger ones with the tell-tale shaved heads, black leather jackets and jackboots worn by all the skinheads back then. It looked like the older guy rode a Harley, and the other two must have shared the second bike, which was almost as noisy because it was old and the timing was off. It was hard to see much because of the light shining straight at the window, so I started for the back bedroom to get a better look.

"Gus, you stay right where you are . . ." Mama said fiercely.

"Don't worry. I'm just going to try and get a better look. You call the police, and I'll get a good description of the men and their bikes."

The old dude got a can of paint and a brush from one of his

saddlebags and started painting something in big strokes along the front of the trailer. The other two just kind of stood around, drinking from a shared bottle and hurling a rock or stick now and then at the trailer, and yelling out cuss words at the top of their lungs. Guess they thought they were something, but I wasn't impressed— watching them, I just felt disgusted. And mad. I wanted to run out there with a bat and chase them off, but Mama had forbidden me to open the door. Also, I couldn't see any weapons, but that didn't mean they didn't have any.

One of the young guys finished the bottle, then took aim and threw it right through the other bedroom window, the one I wasn't peeking through. I didn't think they'd seen me, but I backed away anyway, and went back to the living room. I found Mama standing in the kitchen with the phone receiver held in her hand. She said in a strange voice, "The phone is dead." One of the men must have gone around and cut it on the outside, it was easy enough to find. I remember thinking at the time that it was no big deal, as soon as they were gone I would just bike to the sheriff's office, it wasn't far. But then I noticed that Mama was shaking. She was standing there with a frozen kind of expression I'd never seen before, staring down at the phone and muttering something real low.

"Mama—Mama come sit down," I said. "It's ok. I don't think they're going to come in. They're not going to hurt us, not really."

I don't think she even heard me, but she let me take the phone out of her hand, hang it back up, and lead her over to the couch. She was scared—unreasonable scared, and when I sat her down on the couch she wrapped her arms around herself and started to shake so hard, it was like an earthquake was coming up from inside of her. Under her breath, over and over, she was saying the words, "There's no one to call. There's no one to help." Even though I wasn't too wise in the ways of the world back then, I knew there was more to it than you could account for by the stuff happening in the front yard. Mama was sitting right there next to me, but in reality she was someplace else, somewhere long ago and far away. I tried to put my arm around her and tell her it was going to be all right, but she didn't seem to even know I was there. She just kept shaking and muttering like that for a long time, hunched over and rocking herself like she was in pain.

Meanwhile the three men had gotten back on their bikes and headed off. I wanted to go for the sheriff, but no way was I leaving Mama like that, so I stayed put. I realized after they left that I'd forgotten to write down the numbers of their plates, and the numbers had gone clean out of my head. I was angry at myself. Usually I had a good memory for numbers.

After what seemed like ages, Mama stopped shaking so hard. Then she straightened up and cried for a while, dabbing at her eyes with the tissue I got her. All that time, I just sat there there like a dumbbell, staring down at the carpet, not knowing what to say or do. Eventually she leaned back against the couch with a sigh. She looked thin and worn, and all shrunk into herself like a little child, not like the strong, proud mother I'd always known. I sat next to her, listening to the clock ticking, feeling even more scared than when the men had been outside.

At last I said, "Mama, maybe you'd better tell me about it." It felt like our roles were reversed all of a sudden. Like I was the grown up, and she was the child, needing help. And there was no one there but me. I'd seen a powerful change come over my Mama in the living room that night. I had a few guesses as to what it might mean, but I didn't really know. But I felt we shouldn't just go on like nothing had happened.

She was quiet for a long time, and leaned back with a flat, dull look in her eyes, exhausted. Then she sat up, began folding her tissue in neat little squares, and said softly, "Well, I reckon maybe it's better that you know. Better for me to tell you, than for you to find out some other way. You're old enough now."

"It was my daddy, wasn't it?" I said.

She just nodded.

"He was a bad man, like those men outside, only worse."

She nodded again, and a shudder went all through her body.

I don't know what I had thought all those years. I knew my dad must have been white, and I knew that for some reason Mama had had to run away. Beyond those two facts I'd never really thought. It had never occurred to me that my Mama had been raped.

Rape: It was such an ugly word. I wanted to shove the idea away from me with both hands, before it had time to sink roots into my mind and become real. It must have been horrible for her. She was just a young girl. The same age as I was that night, and the girls I knew from school. Mama looked up at me, and her eyes were as sad as the sea when it rains. "I'm sorry, Gus," she said simply. "It's a hard thing for you to hear about your father. I wish I could tell you he was a different kind of man, but I can't."

But then her expression changed, to her old firmness and resolve, and she said, "But people can change, Gus. People can change. Everybody's made up of partly bad and partly good, including you and me. Sometimes, by the grace of God, the good wins out in a man, and sometimes the bad. But even when they're old, people can change. I don't want you thinkin' bad thoughts about your daddy, Gus, because I figure after all these years you and me have been prayin' for him, he's bound to change. I forgave your daddy long ago, and one day I'm going to see him up in heaven and tell him so. I believe that."

Then she reached over, grabbed my hand, and looked at me hard. "And don't you ever go thinkin' I have any regrets or resentful feelings about the way you came into the world, Gus, because I don't. You're the best thing that ever happened to me. Without you, where would I be now? As soon as I knew I had you, Gus, I knew I had a treasure—something to protect and love, a miracle born out of evil. That gave me hope enough to run away and come here, to make a new life for us, and to give you something better than I ever had. When I told my Momma what had happened, and how I knew I was going' to have a baby, she gave me all she had—all the money she had hidden away for years, sewn up into a mattress, safe from Daddy and his drinking. She was going to use it for herself, but she gave it all to me. And she told me to get as far away as I could from that place, and never look back. So that's what I did. You were my ticket to a new life, Gus. Never for a moment do I regret having you." She let go of my hand and sat back again, and she was back to her old self. Strong and proud—even a bit fierce. But then I guess she'd had to be.

I sat there on the couch, stunned. I tried to look out the window, but the drapes were still closed. It was a lot to take in. At the same time, a lot of things suddenly made sense. I knew it wasn't any good pretending things were different than they really were. That wasn't Mama's way, and it wasn't going to be mine, either. But I also knew that I'd never feel the same inside again, ever. A kind of sad, helpless feeling spread in me. And anger.

Sitting there taking it in, I could feel the heat rising in my body, could hear my heart slamming into my chest. I wanted to go outside, yell my head off, and pound on someone. I wanted to run down those three men on their motorbikes and beat them to a pulp. But they were probably miles down the highway by now, and what could I do? I was just a fourteen year old kid on a bike. I felt angry at God, too. How could he have treated Mama like that? My Mama, probably the best woman in the world, who believed in him more than anyone ever I knew. She never deserved any of it. I remember thinking back then, life sure doesn't make any sense sometimes. I still think that.

But even with my anger running full boil at my so-called father and those three men, I knew Mama wouldn't want me to do anything like the scenarios that were running through my mind. If there was anything she believed in, it was in the goodness of God—and that somehow, in the end, that goodness will come up and swallow everything else. She'd told me stuff like that again and again. Every minute of my life, she showed me a different way. Seeking revenge wasn't right. Instead, men and women were supposed to trust in God. It seemed unnatural, but her example wasn't one I could argue with. How she could forgive a man who hurt her so bad, I didn't understand—but I knew her, and I knew it was for real. At some point down the line, I decided I wanted to live my life the same way. Looking back, I know it didn't happen all at once, it was something that got worked out over a several years. But that night was a definite turning point for me. My life as a child, of taking stuff for granted and just being happy go lucky about everything, was over.

Mama had stopped talking and was sitting now, looking straight out, her face thoughtful and at peace. Then she looked over at me and smiled, and said, "You run along to the Sheriff now, Gus, and tell them what happened. You're itching to go. I'll be all right here."

I jumped off the couch and started for my bike. Then I thought of Mama there alone. "I'll find a phone and call the Foxworthys first. They can come over here and sit with you or something."

"Oh, Gus, you don't have to do that," she said.

"Well I'm going to. They'd be happy to come over. They'd come in a second."

"All right, it doesn't sound like I can talk you out of it anyway," she said, but I was already out the door. I grabbed my bike. Before I took off, I turned to look at what the men had done to the side of the trailer. The word "Nigger" was painted in huge slashing black letters, starting at the bedroom window and stretching across the front door to the living room side. There were dents and dirty scuff-like marks all over the front of the trailer, and both of the bedroom windows were broken. No way should Mama have to sit in there like some woman marked out, to be pointed at and talked about by everyone else in town. I'd tell Mr. Foxworthy to come and get her out of there. I checked my pocket to be sure I had some change, then tore off on my bike as fast as I could for the nearest phone.

Mr. Foxworthy picked me up at the Sheriff's and brought me and my bike back in his truck to get Mama. Then we packed up some clothes and stuff and went home with him. We stayed at the Foxworthys' house for a month until Mr. Foxworthy and some other men from the parish got the phone line and all the windows repaired and the side of the trailer fixed and painted good as new. People talked and whispered as Mama and I walked by, but then they'd always done that. Kids from school asked me about that night, wanting to know what happened, but I brushed them off. It wasn't something I wanted to talk about. The police scouted the area for a week or so and put out a call to all the neighboring towns, but the three men were never caught. Men wearing black leather and riding motorcycles were a dime a dozen on the highway between Lewiston and Missoula in the summertime, and without their license numbers there wasn't much hope of nailing them. I still kick myself over that.

For several months after we moved back into our trailer, Mr. and Mrs. Foxworthy called every night at about nine to check in. But we never had any trouble again.

Part Four: Paul

CHAPTER EIGHTEEN

Gus had a taste for food that was over the top. He liked his sandwiches with three kinds of meat: Turkey, salami, and ham, then layered with slathers of mayonnaise, fat squiggles of mustard, floppy squares of cheese, pickles, onions and hot peppers to boot. He could eat a sandwich with more gusto and self-proclaimed, exaggerated satisfaction than anyone I ever saw. Except he wasn't exaggerating—he really enjoyed it that much. He had a way of throwing his entire self into every experience, of diving headfirst into life, and thinking about the consequences later.

One day we were sitting in Stan's, the pizza and sandwich shop on Main Street. Gus was having his usual, the aforementioned creation. Stan made it especially for him, and never tired of the praise he got from the exuberant Gus. Back when we were in high school, Stan's was the place to hang out. You could sit in a booth and look out at the girls passing by, and there was a room in the back with a few arcade games and an air hockey table. We were talking about our classes, sports, cars, nothing really, when into the booth next to Gus slid a girl.

She was a warm, soft, curvy kind of girl. I recognized her from school, though I'd never talked to her before. She was one of the popular kids. She had long shiny hair and big brown eyes that sparkled as if she were laughing at you—or if not exactly at you, then at something just outside your range that you didn't know about. She was wearing a fluffy pink sweater. I felt my face grow hot, and the hotness spread up toward my ears as I attempted to look up. I knew I wouldn't be able to talk and look in her eyes at the same time, so I looked down into my root beer float instead.

Gus casually lifted his arm, draped it across the girl's shoulders, said, "Hey, Paul, here's someone I've been wanting you to meet. Paul, meet Cheryl. Cheryl, Paul."

"Hi!" she said, in a light, sparkling voice. I felt the crimson creep flushing my cheeks again as I mumbled back hello, and looked up to give what I hoped was a suave grin. She looked amused by my shyness, but not much bothered by it. Then she turned and whispered something to Gus, leaning in close and cupping her hand around his ear. He turned toward her, and then the two of them talked while I stirred at my float with the long spoon, and tried to look occupied. After a few minutes she said she had to go, and slid back out again. "It was great to meet you, Paul," she said.

"Yeah, great," I mumbled, barely looking up.

"Hey Cher, I'll see you tomorrow night. I'll save you a seat," Gus called after her.

"Ok. See you then," she smiled back at him, and then flounced out of the restaurant. Gus watched her walk all the way out the door and down the street with a big, soppy grin smeared across his face.

"Dude! Is she hot, or what?" he said.

"I guess," I mumbled.

"Oh come on, Paul. You've got to admit she's cute. And a real sweetheart, too. I really like this girl."

She was indeed attractive, but I didn't want to admit that to Gus. I tried changing the subject. "I thought we were going to the game tomorrow. With Sam and Henry and the other guys."

"We are. I just invited Cheryl to come along. What's wrong with that?"

"Nothing, I guess. But it won't be the same with a girl around."

"Cher's not just any girl. She's a lot of fun. You'll like her, I promise."

"Whatever you say, Gus. One thing I do know, your Mama won't like it one bit."

"What's not to like? It's no big deal."

"I've heard her say a ton of times that she doesn't want you messing around with girls here in town. She wants you to get good grades and go to college."

"All that stuff is a million years away. What am I supposed to do in the meantime, become a monk?"

"Don't be stupid. All I'm saying is you ought to be careful, you know. You're only a sophomore. You shouldn't get tied up with a girl yet."

Gus was getting defensive. "So who appointed you to be my watch dog? Can't a guy have a little fun without the town Preacher's Kid getting his back up about it?"

That stung and he knew it. If there was anything I hated about my life, it was that I was the town Preacher's kid.

"Well I know you, Gus," I shot back. "I know you better than almost anyone. And you don't think sometimes. You just do stuff and then you're in a mess, and then guess who has to get you out of it?"

Gus finished the last bite of his sandwich, gulped the rest of his soda, and slid out of the booth, grabbing his jacket. As he did so, he clapped his hand on my shoulder. "Hey," he said, "Don't worry. This time, I'll think." He flashed his most charming smile at me, but I shrugged his hand off. Inside, a little egg of worry had hatched in my mind. I'd grown up with Gus, and I knew how impulsive he could be, how completely clueless he was about the consequences that followed his impulses, and how quickly he could get himself into trouble.

And I won't deny I was also more than a little jealous. All of a sudden, Gus had a girlfriend, and I hadn't even known.

CHAPTER NINETEEN

After that, we saw Cheryl more and more. It seemed like whenever we went to Stan's, or the park, or school, or a game, there she'd be. Gus was never one to ditch a friend—he liked to have anyone and everyone around. But sometimes I couldn't help but wish she wasn't there. Still, Gus was right, she was pretty cool for a girl. Not bossy or prissy, or needing attention every minute like some girls. She didn't seem to mind doing guy stuff, like watching a game or shooting baskets. After a while, we were like a threesome, and I could even look her in the eye and talk like normal because she was Gus's girl—more like an extension of him than a girl you'd get all flustered about. Everything seemed all right. But there were still times when, in the back of my mind, it worried me. And Gus's Mama, she was worrying more and more.

When I saw Mrs. Kenover back then, she often had a stern, pinched look, like she was biting her lower lip, thinking hard. Or, more likely, praying. Sometimes when we were all together, she'd look at Gus—just look at him, steady and unblinking, and we all knew what she was thinking, because she made no secret of her disapproval of the idea of Gus having a girlfriend. She liked Cheryl well enough, she just thought he was too young to be dating anyone. Even Gus the oblivious would notice and squirm a bit, when she looked at him like that. But then he'd start teasing, cracking jokes, and making big of everything, and Mrs. Kenover would forget herself and laugh.

I went over to Gus's house almost every day, sometimes when he wasn't even there. I couldn't stand it at my house, so if Gus was out, I would sit at the kitchen table and do homework, or even climb up and sit in the fort and just think. One afternoon after yet another fight with my Mom, I went over to find Gus, and ended up talking with Mrs. Kenover instead.

"But I can't stand her," I said. "I hate her whining and nagging at us all the time. I hate her always asking about my day, prying into my life. I wish she'd just leave me alone. At least when I come here there's some peace."

"Paul, you just think about your poor Mama. She looks after you, your little brother, your Dad, and the house. She takes care of the whole lot of you the whole day through. But who looks after your Mama? Whoever thinks about her?"

I thought about it for a minute, and then I said, "I guess nobody thinks about her."

"That's right," said Mrs. Kenover. "And she's bound to get tired and worn out, and you're the oldest son. You ought to think about these things. You ought to think about what you can do to lighten her load, instead of just complaining about your own."

So I went home that night, and I tried. I tried to say cheerful things, and ask how her day was, and stuff like that. She just looked back at me with a withering, suspicious look. At first I felt angry, but then I realized that probably nobody had asked her anything like that for a long, long time. One day I came home and found her standing in the kitchen, a dishtowel hanging forgotten in her hand, just staring into space. Awkwardly, impulsively, I gave her a kiss on the cheek. She looked at me as if in shock, dropped her dishtowel, and started to cry. I even started helping with dishes after supper once in a while on nights when Father wasn't home. Having company seemed to cheer her up, so at least she didn't bang about so much. But we didn't talk much. I never knew what to say, and maybe she didn't either.

By the time I was in high school, things at home had gone from bad to worse. Sometimes Dad would leave the house right after dinner without even saying a word, and not return until late at night when we were all in bed. Instead of arguing and getting upset like she did before, Mom just seemed to get quieter and quieter. Once in a while she would burst into tears for what seemed like no reason at all, in the middle of dinner, or cooking, or just anything. And then she would go shut herself in her room. She would come out afterward, with her hair combed and her face washed. I hinted a few times that maybe she could go visit Mrs. Kenover, like the old times, but she just shook her head. She hardly left the house anymore, and she always seemed afraid—jumping and startling at the slightest sound. Sometimes she didn't even go to church on Sundays, claiming that she had a headache, or didn't feel well. And more and more, my father just left her alone.

CHAPTER TWENTY

It was a Saturday afternoon in late summer, right before my senior year. I'd looked all over town for Gus, and finally found him and Cheryl sitting behind the equipment shed in the playing fields at the back of the high school. I jogged over and yelled, "Hey, what's up?"

They both stopped talking and Gus turned toward me. Cheryl didn't look up, and Gus didn't smile. I could tell Cher was crying, and Gus had hold of her hand. I backed away, apologizing, and they returned to their quiet, furtive talking as if I wasn't even there.

I felt hurt, left out, and angry. Guess I'd just have to find someone else to hang out with for the day, I thought. But I couldn't help but wonder what was going on. I went back to Mrs. Kenover's trailer and found her in the middle of a pile of ironing. I grabbed an apple, flopped down on the old green sofa, and said, "What's up with Gus? I found him and Cheryl talking in the schoolyard, and he would hardly even look up at me."

Mrs. Kenover looked up. She set the iron aside, shutting it off automatically, then came over to her rocker and picked up her knitting, looking distracted. It wasn't like her to be distracted. She had the same tight expression I often saw on her face then, a mixture of worry and earnest prayer. Mrs. Kenover was the only person I ever met who could be carrying on a conversation with God himself right in the middle of chores, cooking, or even while talking to you.

"Now, I don't rightly know," she said. "Something must be wrong, if he wouldn't talk to you. Let's just wait here and see."

We didn't have to wait long. About twenty minutes later Gus's heavy feet sounded on the steps and he came in, letting the screen door slam shut behind him. He walked straight over to his mother. I don't think he ever even noticed me sitting there in the room. Later Gus told me that that was the hardest thing he ever had to do—to walk up to that godly woman, with her deep brown eyes fixed gravely upon him, and tell her that he, in rebellion to the ways of God and despite all his Mama's wise warnings, had caused a girl to become pregnant. And the two of them not even graduated from school.

But he did it. He came in to the house and she dropped her knitting in her lap, maybe guessing already that the thing she most dreaded to hear was true. He walked up to her chair and knelt own, so filled with shame that he couldn't even look up, he just kept his eyes glued to the carpet. The he said, in a whisper, "Mama—I did something so bad!" And then he choked on his words. Then those mother hands reached out and took the head of her almost-grown boy, and holding it on her lap she said, "There, there, boy. I know what you've done." And Gus started weeping like a baby. He cried so hard his breath came in giant heaves and moans. And all the time Mrs. Kenover patted him and said, "There, there, now. It's going to be all right."

When he was all cried out she lifted up his face so her eyes looked right into his and she said, "Well, I s'pose that's how it is with most of us men and women. All of us like stubborn mules. We've got to be broken before we can learn. We're all prodigals, one way or another—running from the sin inside of us, or running from the sins of others and the ways they try to destroy us. Every last one of us needing to run home."

"Now Gus," she said, "You are goin' to be a man. Not like your father. You are goin' to be a man and marry this girl, and finish school and find a job and support the lot of you. Granted, things are going to be harder because of this. But I'll be there to help and Jesus will be there to help, and I know you'll make it through. You all can live with me when the baby comes, and I'll take care of it while you two finish up school. I know all about babies, and I reckon poor Cheryl doesn't know a thing. Though she'll learn right quick, just like I had to do with you."

Gus nodded, then spoke softly, "Yes, Mama." Then he repeated, "Yes, Mama. I will. But Cher's Daddy isn't going to like it one bit. He's never liked me at all."

"No, he won't," said Mrs. Kenover. "But he'll just have to accept it, in time. The girl is going to have to make a choice, and I reckon her way will be with you."

Gus nodded slowly, taking it all in. "Mama?" he asked, "I think I'd better go find Cheryl. She was awful upset when I left."

"All right Gus, if you think that's best," she said. She walked him to the door. "I'll see you when you come home then," she said.

"Okay," he said distractedly, rushing away with his new preoccupation, forgetting to give her the kiss on the cheek he always gave her when he went out. Mrs. Kenover sighed and closed the door softly behind him, then returned to her chair and started rocking, and put her face in her hands. Probably she was praying.

I crept out the door and replaced the latch as quietly as I could, unnoticed and unmissed. Then I walked home the long way, along the river, my mind crammed full of all the things I'd just seen and heard. I didn't feel like going home, so I stayed out till I heard the chirping and creaking of the crickets start up above the noise of the water as the sun sank down below the mountains. The light softened and faded, a coolness cut through the air, and the river turned from the color of dull metal to a dark inky blue, and at last I walked home.

CHAPTER TWENTY-ONE

The wedding was a month later, with Father Johnston officiating. I was the best man. When Gus made his vows to Cheryl, I could tell that he meant them in a way that he had hardly meant anything before. I could see Mrs. Kenover's eyes shining with tears of both pride and sadness for her son. Mom and Jeremy were there, and Mr. and Mrs. Foxworthy. Cher's Dad walked his daughter down the aisle with a grim face, and her mom wore a frozen-in-place-smile. They both left right afterward.

Gus and Cheryl went to a fancy restaurant up in Coeur d'Alene and splurged on a night at a hotel. Then they moved in to Gus's old room in the Kenover's trailer, and returned to school on Monday almost like normal. But not really normal at all. Gus was with Cheryl almost all the time, and soon lost his reputation for being the life of the party. When the other kids talked about parties and dates and football games, he was quiet. Gus took an after-school job at the IGA. He hoped to work his way up from a box boy to checker, and he worked most Friday and Saturday nights. Joey

Larson, the manager of the store, went to the Catholic Church and was a longtime friend of Mrs. Kenover's, delivering her groceries special. Gus was hard working, quick, and cheerful, and the managers liked him.

Of course, people talked. But people had always talked. Mrs. Kenover simply didn't acknowledge rude comments, sidelong looks, or prying questions. She just acted as polite as ever, and kept to herself like she always had. Only rarely did a person see her running errands in town. Sometimes I wondered if she ever got lonely. Thinking back, I'm sure she must have felt lonely or down sometimes, if she ever gave herself permission to think about it. But if she did, she sure never let it show.

By late Fall, around homecoming, Cher had started to bloom out, and her tight sweaters and painted on jeans were replaced with balloon-style shirts and loose dresses. But she held her head high, and Gus treated her like a queen. If the other kids made mean remarks, they didn't do it where either of them could hear. Gus had a short, stocky build, had made it to the state finals in wrestling, and was known for his short fuse.

I imagine living with Mrs. Kenover was good for Cheryl. She didn't seem to know a thing about simple stuff like how to boil an egg or clean a toilet, things even my mom had taught me. Sometimes when I was over in the evenings, it seemed like the two of them were in the middle of formal lessons. Mrs. Kenover was not the most patient of teachers, and Cher was slow to learn to say the least. The four of us endured more than one supper of rock-hard biscuits, gravy with lumps, and burnt pies. Gus could turn a meal like that into a regular stand-up comedy routine, and Cheryl had the kind of personality to laugh and take it well. Even though they were way too young to be married, they were a good match.

Meanwhile, things at my house were even worse. My brother Jeremy was constantly in trouble at school, getting in fights and picking on the smaller kids. The school kept calling our house and threatening to expel him. My mother would get on the phone and plead for one more chance. My father blamed the school, blamed my mother, blamed the devil, and wouldn't come to the phone at all.

CHAPTER TWENTY-TWO

It seemed to me, looking on from the outside, that my father was a cold man, his chest hard and empty as a square steel box. Always, he had to be *right*. His God was a God of righteousness, of unwavering standards, of vindication. Every thought or action had its rightful consequence, its full explanation. When I was little, I feared him—I cringed beneath the lectures and the spankings. But when I grew older, my fear turned to hate. I hated what he did to us, to my mother and brother. I hated his false show of concern for his church members, his faked interest in their illnesses and their problems. To me it seemed all for show: Part of the minister's costume that he put on each Sunday morning, and shed as soon as he walked inside his own front door.

As I grew older, I didn't demonstrate the proper show of respect that a son should, and the long, emotionless lectures and pious explanations of my boyhood turned into blind rages and spectacular explosions of anger. After such episodes, he would lock himself in his study for hours. Once I even thought I heard him crying. But I told myself if he was miserable, it was only what he deserved.

My mother didn't dare argue with him anymore. She came into my room once after one of his rages, and sat down on the edge of my bed. I was lying on my stomach doing homework, and I didn't look up. After a long time, she said, "What's going to happen to us, Paul?" I shrugged. I didn't know, and I didn't care. I thought anything would be better than what was. Little did I know then how soon our whole world would explode like a shot out of a gun, would lie like a litter of shrapnel spread across the ground. This is the way it all fell out.

One Saturday morning that same fall, I came back to the house early. My Mom had stopped her visiting routine long ago, but we kids were supposed to stay out of the house on Saturday mornings; that was the rule. Father needed peace and quiet to prepare for Sunday, or so we had always been told. But some of the guys were going to play ball and I needed my mitt, so I went back to the house to look for it. I looked in the garage, in my room, in the family room, and I still couldn't find it. I knocked on the door of my father's study and opened it to ask if he had seen it anywhere, and . . . there was a woman there. It was the church secretary, Miss Briggs. My father was in his chair, which was pushed back from his desk, and she was sitting on his lap with her arms around his neck. She was wearing a bright blue, filmy kind of dress, which she quickly pulled down over her knees.

My father stood up, shoving her away from him. His face

turned fire-engine red, livid with rage. He yelled at me, "How many times have I told you that you are never to enter this room on Saturday mornings? GET OUT!"

But I didn't get out. At least not immediately. I stood there, fascinated, as the scene in front of me engraved itself in my mind so that I can recall every detail to this day. I can see father's study with its shelves of commentaries, books and bibles, and the framed family portrait hanging dead center over his desk. And Miss Briggs standing there awkwardly in her stocking feet, with her fake-blond hair, her hot pink lipstick and nails, and her eyes looking anywhere but at me. And I can still see my father glowering at me with hatred and rage and then—fear.

I closed the door and walked out of the house without my mitt. I went to the place by the river where Gus and I used to go to talk serious talk, or just to mess around, before he had a girlfriend. I sat down and looked out at the river and listened to it rushing past like it always did, on and on, with never any change or any relief. And I knew I had the evidence to ruin him—to tear down his precious Christian reputation, to smear his face in the mud. But suddenly all I could think of was my mother, coming in and sitting so quiet on the edge of my bed sometimes at night. Of all her efforts to pretend that we were a normal, happy Christian family.

I sat there for the rest of the afternoon, replaying the events of the morning over and over in my head until the sun fell low in the sky and the cold began to creep up from the ground. The river sped past below, swift and gray. I tried to pray, but nothing happened. If

God didn't speak to me at a time like this, I thought, what's the use of praying at all? If God even did speak to people. I wasn't convinced that he did. Part of me suspected that the whole God-and-Jesus story wasn't actually real, was just another way for one group of people to get another group of people to do what they wanted them to do. Whether God was really up there, looking down and caring about what happens to people—I guess it would be nice for us if he was, but as far as I was concerned the jury was out.

Dinner that night was eaten in silence. My mother tried a couple of times to make conversation, asking what everyone did that day, asking about the topic of tomorrow's sermon, but nobody even tried to answer. Father did not look up from his plate, nor I from mine. Jeremy slouched, leaning on his elbow with his big feet sticking out on either side of his chair. He started poking finger holes in his mashed potatoes and was sent up to his room. I went up immediately after dinner to sit and stare at my math book, but ended up looking out the window, spinning a pen around my index finger, and drawing rows of little boxes across the top of my page. I couldn't concentrate to do my homework. I wanted to go down and watch TV, but I didn't want to see my dad. Around nine thirty I heard the door slam, the sound of my mother yelling something, and the engine of our Oldsmobile starting up and driving away.

Half an hour later I crept downstairs. My mother was sitting on the couch, staring straight out in front of her, in shock. I sat across from her in the recliner—my father's chair—and looked down at the floor. I didn't know if he had told her, and I knew she had to know.

"I saw him, Mom. In the study with Miss Briggs."

She turned her head and stared toward me, her face blank, uncomprehending.

"She was there in the study. She was on his lap. She was *with* him."

There was silence. Her face, lit by the table lamp, was like the shell of an egg; smooth and expressionless and white.

"If I ever see him again, I'll kill him. That fucking asshole. That jerk . . . ." I said bitterly, the dammed up hate pouring out of my mouth like a river of black.

"Paul!" my mother said to me sharply, "Don'tt talk about your father like that. I will not stand for it."

"But he lied to us, Mom. He lied to us. He put on this pious, holier-than-God-Himself act, and all along he . . ."

"Go to your room."

Her face was firm, resolved, even fierce.

"I'm almost 18 now. You can't tell me what to do."

"Go to your room," she repeated.

I got up and then I stood there, shaking with anger. I wanted to start screaming, to throw things, to make her understand. But her face was turned away from me, looking out the window at the dark night. She was like a statue carved out of stone, her eyes narrowed, her face set, and her mouth pressed tight in a thin line.

So I went upstairs like she said. I laid in bed and threw a rubber ball up at the ceiling, hearing the thunk, thunk of it, until I threw it too hard and it bounced onto the floor and rolled away. I wished Gus was home so I could go over there, but he was working late that night stocking shelves or something. Eventually, I must have gone to sleep, because I woke up Monday morning in the same clothes.

CHAPTER TWENTY-THREE

The next morning, after the organist had completed the last notes of the hymn of invocation and everyone had sat down, my mother walked bravely up to the front and stood, clutching the pulpit with both hands. She looked out to the small congregation, took a deep, quavering breath, and said, "My husband has left. The secretary, Miss Briggs, might have gone with him. I . . . I suppose that's all I have to tell you. I . . . suppose I'll be leaving soon, too."

And then she broke down. She gave a great, pitiful, choking sob, said, "Oh, God!" and put her hands up over her face. One of the elders sitting nearby got up, took her arm, and walked her back to our pew. And then there she sat between Jeremy and myself, crying harder and harder, and not even trying to stop. The sound of it echoed through the high-ceilinged room. For a minute, the rest of the church sat in stunned silence. I could hear the sound of the dry autumn leaves rustling in the breeze, coming through the open windows on the sides.

The chairman of the board of Elders walked up to the pulpit and announced awkwardly that service was canceled for the day, and everyone was dismissed. The congregation looked at each other uncertainly, then slowly got up and shuffled out the back doors, looking over their shoulders at us and whispering. A few people walked up to my mother first and tried patting her on the arm, or mumbling something sympathetic, but she didn't even look up. Jeremy and I sat in our stiff Sunday shirts, looking down at the floor and our shoes. I wondered if he even understood what was happening. He was only twelve years old. Then I noticed he was making gouges with the point of a penknife into the wood of the pew seat. The few who came up to us glared at him in consternation, but nobody told him to stop.

A few of the elders waited in the back until the church had emptied out, then walked Mom to our car. I drove home, walked my mother over to the couch, and then Jeremy and I both went up to our separate rooms. Then I just lay on my bed, looking out the window at a pale bleached sky, listening to the trees in the gusting wind.

About an hour later, Mrs. Kenover came. She knocked quietly and then let herself in, and went to sit by Mother on the couch. Mom was still crying loudly, ungracefully, her face all red and blotchy, blowing her nose into her already soaked tissue. Mrs. Kenover sat next to her and put her arm around Mom's bent shoulders. Eventually she got Mom to quiet down, and walked her upstairs to her bed. Then she came back down and made some lunch.

While the three of us, Mrs. Kenover, me and Jeremy, sat at the table with plates of tuna sandwiches and chocolate milk, I told her, "If I ever see that fucking jerk again, I'm going to kill him. I'll kill him for what he did to us. He doesn't even deserve to live."

Mrs. Kenover looked hard at me for a long time. Her eyes were ancient and sad and flashing angry, all at the same time. Then she said, "That would be a foolish, foolish thing to do. It's foolish to even think that way. Don't you see? That wouldn't help anything. Paul, you're no better than him, and you know it."

"Him?" I said indignantly, "Him?! He's never loved us. He's never loved anyone. He's the coldest man I ever met, and what's worse, he hides the fact behind a big Christian act. Just about anyone is better than him."

"No they aren't," she insisted. "You aren't and I'm not and Gus isn't and nobody is. You look deep into your heart, and you'll see. All our good works are like filthy rags. There is none righteous, the Bible says. Not even one. Without the grace of Jesus, we're none of us better than a filthy rag. The way of Jesus is not the way of revenge."

The last thing on earth I wanted to hear right then was a sermon. I groaned and rolled my eyes, but Mrs. Kenover ignored me and kept right on. "You keep thinkin' those thoughts about your Pa, Paul—those hate-filled thoughts, and you'll become just like him, or even worse. Bitter and angry and filled with hate. You think about these things, because I'm telling you the truth. History repeats itself in families, but history can be broken through the shed blood of

Jesus. And Paul, I know you don't want to become like your Pa."

She had me on that one. If there was anything I didn't want, it was that. I started to listen, a little.

"See, unless you forgive," she said, "It doesn't work. There's just hate building on hate—more and more hate, and no way to break free."

I didn't have anything to say to that. Maybe she was right, but all I knew right then was that anger was pumping through my veins like wildfire, ready to boil up out of me and explode. Mrs. Kenover turned her attention to Jeremy, who as usual was mutilating his food instead of eating it. I felt I had to get away from the house. Away from her, away from my father, away from all of it. I picked up my plate and glass, threw out the uneaten half of my sandwich, and put them in the sink. Then I left without a word, not even a thank you for the lunch. Mrs. Kenover went to the door and called out after me, but I didn't look back. I just kept walking.

CHAPTER TWENTY-FOUR

I sat and looked out at the river for a long time, watching the light change from pale white to colder and colder blue and finally black. It was like someone walked up, put a giant mouth up to the sky, and sucked in all the brightness. Then, holding it all inside their chest, they turned around and walked away. I lay on my back in the matted grass and looked up through the branches of the trees at the stars coming out. The air had the bite of winter in it, and I was cold, I hadn't brought a jacket. But the chill in the air matched the way I felt on the inside, so I just kept lying there, letting the cold from the earth seep right up into my bones.

Gus came. He walked up and sat down next to me, and started to light a cigarette.

"Thought you told Cheryl you were going to quit," I said.

He looked down at it. "You're right," he said, and flicked it, glowing, into the water. One hot wink in the darkness, and the river carried it away. We sat together for a long time, not saying anything,

Gus looking out at the river, me looking up at the stars. Then Gus broke the silence.

"Mama told me," he said.

"I figured," I answered.

"She said you were taking it kind of hard."

"How would you take it?" I asked, feeling the hot anger rising up in my chest again, displacing all the cold from the ground.

"Your Dad is . . . ," Gus said, hesitating. "Well, maybe it's better he's gone."

I nodded. That was obvious. Then there was silence again for a long time.

"Your Mama says I have to forgive him," I choked out at last.

"My Mama's never wrong," he said simply.

"Yeah, well, how the hell am I supposed to do that? Just forgive him, just like that? Just forget about all the years he yelled at us, the way he treated us? I hate him. And I can't even imagine feeling anything else."

Gus started for a cigarette again, then thought better of it, and chucked the whole pack into the river. He shrugged and said, "I don't know. You just have to do it, that's all. You say to yourself, I'm going to forgive him, and then you do it. Then when it comes up again, you have to tell yourself again, and keep on doing it.

Sometimes you have to do stuff you don't feel."

Everything was always so simple for him. Here's the problem, here's what you do. Just do it and don't think too hard about it, and go on your way a'whistlin'. It's one of the ways we were different. Nothing was ever simple for me. Life felt dark and tangled, encroaching in all around me like the twisted branches of the trees overhead, blocking out the light of most of the stars.

"So, you mean to tell me you've forgiven *your* dad?"

Gus thought for a few minutes, then said, "Yeah, I guess I have. I haven't thought about it for a while now. When I first found out what he was like, I hated him, just like you hate your Pa now. Mama said I had to forgive him, and I didn't think I ever could. But with the baby coming, I guess I had a change of heart. I messed up so bad—who am I not to forgive anyone?"

"It's not like you raped Cheryl, Gus. There's a big difference between you and your dad, whoever he is."

"Yeah, but . . . it's hard to explain. Things changed and I changed. Or I'm changing, I hope. Mama forgave me. I mean, she could've kicked us both out. I just about broke her heart, and I hate myself for it sometimes. She could have been like Cher's parents, mad at us all the time, barely even able to look at us. But look at all she's doing, helping us get through school, sticking by us when things are tough. So what I mean is, I'm not exactly qualified to hold out on anyone else. It's like that part in the Bible, where a guy owes his master like, a million bucks. And his master forgives the whole thing. Then the guy goes out and beats up some other guy who owes him like, ten bucks."

"Great. Now I get a sermon from you, too. I don't need to be preached at, Gus. I've had it my whole life. You're just as bad as your Mama."

That riled him. "You watch how you talk about Mama, Paul. She's been good to you. I won't have you saying anything against her. Argue with me about God all you want, but leave her out of it."

I felt like a rat. Part of me didn't even care what I said, but Gus was right. His Mama was untouchable. If anyone had earned the right to say what they believed about God and be respected for it, it was her. And the last thing I needed now was to get Gus all mad at me.

"Sorry," I said. "I didn't really mean it. My dad was such a Bible thumper, always pounding it in to us. It's just a little hard to take sometimes. When someone starts spouting Bible verses, I think of him."

Gus got up, brushing the dirt and pine needles off his jeans. "Well, I gotta go. I told Cher I'd be back in an hour. I still have a paper to write for history."

"Ok. Catch you later," I said.

He hesitated, looking down at me. "You oughtta go too, Paul. It's freezing out."

"I can take care of myself. I'll go home when I feel like it."

He stood there looking down at me for a minute longer. I closed my eyes. "All right then. See you later," he said, and jogged off down the trail toward his house. A few minutes later, I got up and jogged the opposite way down the same trail. Bus was right, it was freezing out. And suddenly, I realized I was hungry.

CHAPTER TWENTY-FIVE

I found Mom on the couch wrapped up in a blanket, her hands around a mug of hot chocolate. "Mrs. Kenover just left to get some groceries," she said. "She'll be back in half an hour to make dinner."

I sat down across from my mom, not knowing what to say. She looked like a cat, sitting there all curled up inside herself, staring out into space. After a few minutes I asked, "Where's Jeremy?"

"Mrs. Kenover took him with her to help carry. Did you see Gus?

"Yeah," I said.

"Do you have any homework to finish before school tomorrow?"

"Just some reading. I can do it later."

We sat there quiet in the dim room. It was only 7:00, but it was pitch black outside.

"Mom?" I said awkwardly. "It's going to be all right. We might even be better off than before."

"Oh, Paul," she said, and she started tearing up again, but only a little. I handed her a tissue. She blew her nose and tucked it into her waistband to save for later. "You might be right. But it's all so overwhelming. We'll have to find a place to live." Her voice quavered. We lived in the parsonage owned by the church. Except for the years when Father had gone to seminary, my mother had never lived anywhere else.

She reached over and put her empty mug on an end table, then said softly, looking down and fingering the fringe of the blanket with her hands, "I really loved your father, once. It hasn't been like that for a long, long time, but he was different, in the beginning— back before we came to this place. Somehow things changed, he changed, and I never understood why. But I wish you could have known him like he was before. He wasn't always the way you remember him."

We heard Mrs. Kenover and Jeremy coming in through the back door, and the door slamming shut from the wind. "Good Lord, what a night!" Mrs. Kenover called out, as she walked into the living room to hang their coats in the closet. "There's a storm blowing in. I brought my night things in case it was too rough to walk home later. Now, I'll just put on some tinned soup and biscuits, it will only take a few minutes. Cheryl handed me a movie for the VCR she thought you all might like as I was walking out. Paul, maybe you can put this in, and you can watch while I cook. I've never tried to work one of those new machines."

"Sure," I said. It was a Bill Murray comedy. Father would have never allowed us to watch it. But Father wasn't here.

That night in bed I stayed awake for a long time, thinking about my mom and dad. I'd seen a few pictures of them when they were young. Their wedding picture, a few photos with friends they used to have, and a few from when I was a baby. Mom was young and pretty and slim—she'd always been slim—and in some of the pictures my dad was smiling. It was hard to imagine him being young and happy. I hadn't seen him smile for years and years.

Had he ever smiled at me? There were a few times when he was proud. Once when I had recited a poem perfectly in the 4th grade assembly, or when my report cards were good. He seemed sort of happy then. On my birthdays, he would always say a long prayer before we cut the cake. It was boring, and to a young boy it seemed to last a whole eternity. But it seemed like he meant the things he prayed then, like he was glad to have me for a son. Then he would hand me a crisp twenty dollar bill I could use to buy anything I wanted. We never had a lot of money, so twenty dollars felt like a lot.

We took a vacation to the Oregon coast once, right before Jeremy was born. It's one of the earliest things I can remember. I remember him taking me down to the shoreline and standing there, watching me run in and out of the waves. We built a fort in the sand with a huge moat all around it. It's the only time I can remember him playing with me. I was maybe four or five years old.

I wondered where he was now, and if Miss Briggs was with him. Would they go to a hotel? What would they do? He couldn't exactly apply for a new job as a minister somewhere—no one would take him. As I fell asleep, I wondered if Miss Briggs was still wearing the same filmy blue dress and nylon stockings. And I wondered if I would ever see my father again.

CHAPTER TWENTY-SIX

About a month later we sat, the six of us, in Mrs. Kenover's living room: Me, my mom, Jeremy, Gus, Cheryl, and of course Mrs. Kenover. We were eating homemade pie, and it wasn't bad. Mrs. Kenover must have really worked with Cher on her crusts.

"Hey Jeremy," Gus said, "Come to my room and I'll show you something."

"What?" Jeremy asked suspiciously.

"Only the latest issue of *Aviation Week* magazine. I picked it up in Spokane a few weeks ago."

"Awesome!" said Jeremy, lighting up like a firecracker. Jeremy was crazy about planes. His one ambition in life was to be an Air Force fighter pilot.

"Come on back, and I'll show it to you," Gus said, then leaned over the couch and gave Cher a noisy smack on the lips, and rubbed her belly. "See ya later, little Fred."

Gus had taken to calling the baby little Fred. Don't ask me why. He could be so mushy sometimes, it was embarrassing. But Cher just laughed at him. Gus had made a point lately of hanging out with Jeremy sometimes, kind of taking the kid under his wing. I think his Mama put him up to it. However it happened, Jeremy was all over it, lapping it up like a starving puppy, and he seemed to be coming around a little. Gus knew how to talk with him about planes and engines and battles and stuff like that, and somehow he had managed to talk to him some about bullies, and get him to understand a bit how it felt on the other side. The school hadn't called our house all month. Gus was great at relating with kids. Maybe because he was the type of guy who never really does grow up.

Mom and Mrs. Kenover were talking. Mom said, "I don't know what to do or where to go. The church board is letting us stay until they find a new Pastor, but we'll have to leave soon. I want to find somewhere far away, where I don't have to face anyone."

"Where will you go?" Mrs. Kenover asked.

"I don't know. My parents passed away years ago, and I'm not very close to my sisters. It's been so long."

They were quiet for a few minutes, Mom looking down into her coffee cup, and Mrs. Kenover looking at Mom, thinking. Then Mrs. Kenover said, "If you want my advice—and I know you're not asking for it—I think you should stay right here, where people know you and care about you and can help. It would be hard to go off to a new place where nobody knows who you are, and start all over again. Too many changes all at once. It would be hard on your boys."

"But that's what you did," my Mom said.

"Yes, but I was fourteen and too young to know any better. And I had no other good options. God took care of me when I needed him to. He'll do the same for you."

"But I feel so embarrassed and ashamed. I hate going out to the shops and running into people I know. Everywhere I go in this town, I see someone. How can I face people from church?"

"You face them just as you are—lonely and vulnerable and not hiding a thing. And mark my words, they'll take you into their hearts, at least some of them will. They'll see your bravery and admire you for it. And some of them might even come and tell you their own troubles, things they never could tell anyone before."

Mother sighed and was quiet. The future looked hard and bleak. But in that little trailer surrounded by friends, it felt a little more endurable.

The week following, a lawyer in our town, a man from our church, offered to train Mom to work in his office as a legal secretary. After her first day of work, she barely made it through the front door before she ran to her room, and I could hear her crying, and saying out loud, "God, I can't do this! I'm too old for this! Why should I have to start all over again?!"

She emerged about an hour later, her face puffy but

composed. She got out the bread, and started spreading peanut butter on open slices, making sandwiches for dinner. "Uh, how did it go?" I asked.

"Terrible," she said, her voice cracking. "They want me to learn to type, and file, and how to use a computer of all things. And I have lists of legal words to study, and all this technical stuff to read that I don't even understand. Worst of all, I have to be shown how to do everything just like I'm a little child."

She started to break down again. A tear splashed down onto one of the slices of bread spread with peanut butter, and sat there quivering like a little globe.

"I know how to do some of that stuff, Mom. If we can find someone with a computer, I can show you how to do that at least."

"You can?" she said, surprised.

"Sure. We use computers all the time at school. They're easy."

Mom heaved a big sigh, and tried to smile as she stuck the tops on the sandwiches, and got out a jug of milk. "Well, maybe if you could show me a few things, I won't feel quite so dumb. I'm afraid I'm not what they expected, or need, at all."

"Sure," I said. "I think Henry's dad has a computer. I'll call and see if we can go tonight."

"Tonight?" she said, her eyes wide. "Oh Paul, you can't call on such short notice. I don't want to impose. Don't ask about tonight."

But I was already punching the numbers on the phone. Mrs. Banks answered and said that it would be no problem, they weren't using the computer that night and didn't have any plans.

"Told you so," I said. Mom just pressed her lips together and looked white.

We walked over after dinner. Mr. Banks led us back to the family room and lifted the dust cover off the machine. It was one of the old Dos computers, a 386, where you had to know all the right codes and keys to press. We practiced each step—booting up the computer, getting into the word processing program, typing a few lines, and then shutting it down—several times until Mom felt comfortable doing it by herself. She took a ton of notes, her neat, cramped handwriting forming a perfect rectangle that covered half a page in a spiral notebook. It didn't really take long at all, and after a while Mr. and Mrs. Banks came back to check on our progress.

"Sarah, you're so brave. I've never even touched the computer," said Mrs. Banks, a plump woman in her late forties with dyed red hair.

"They're quite simple, Mona, once you get the hang of them," said her husband. "I ought to teach you. Then we could transfer our checking account and whatnot onto it. Make life easier."

"You can do that using WordPerfect?" asked Mom.

"No, there's other programs that you use for numbers called

spreadsheets. I read recently that they're even selling a program all set up to run your checking account, so all you have to do is type in the amount of your deposits and checks, and the computer does all the rest. You can label your expenses and keep track of a budget that way."

"Well, maybe it's good I'm learning now," said Mom.

"Yes," said Mrs. Banks, "They say pretty soon we'll be doing everything by computer—reading books, shopping, even taking classes instead of going to school. I can't imagine doing all of that just sitting at a machine, but I suppose you never know. Paul, you must be a good teacher. Maybe I should hire you to teach me some afternoon."

I shrugged and said, "It's no big deal."

"New ways of doing things come easier to you younger ones, though," Mrs. Banks said. Then she asked Mom, "Sarah, how do you like your new job?"

"Oh, today was my first day," she said, then laughed—a genuine laugh. "Actually it was terrible. Mr. Oldham was so patient, but everything is just new to me. I've never worked in an office, or in any job at all."

"Well, I think you're very brave, staying here in town and doing what you're doing. I admire you."

"You do?" Mom asked incredulously.

"Yes, we all do. Don't we, Harold?"

Mr. Banks gave a firm nod, and said, "Yes. Nobody knew how you would take it, when Pastor up and left like that. But here you are, holding your head up, and getting along just fine."

"Oh," Mom said, turning pink. "I don't feel like I'm doing so well. Sometimes I think everyone must be laughing at me."

"Not at all!" Mrs. Banks said. "Why, just the other day I was talking to . . ."

At that point I could tell they were going to talk for a while, so I waved to Mom and slipped out the back door. I'd hoped to catch Henry and shoot some hoops, but he was out with his girlfriend. Seemed like the whole stinking world had a girlfriend all of a sudden. I couldn't imagine getting myself tied down like that. I liked my freedom, and I also liked my space. And the one thought I held in my mind that year above all others was that I was going to be leaving soon. College was the oasis on my horizon. It meant getting out on my own, with all new people, all new surroundings. And I could hardly wait.

CHAPTER TWENTY-SEVEN

Winter passed, cold and rainy and gray. Usually it snows more in the mountains, but not that year. I was busy with all the senior year stuff, applying for colleges and for every scholarship I could track down that I might possibly qualify for, and working for a remodeling contractor after school to save money. Mom was busy with her new job, and banged away on the old typewriter in my dad's study practicing her typing most evenings. Jeremy dodged both of us, and spent his evenings holed up in his room with his comic books and model planes, except for the rare occasions when Gus came over and forced him out. Mom nagged Jeremy to invite a friend over from school, but he didn't seem to have any. But he didn't seem to be getting into trouble all the time any more.

On one of the rare days he was off work, Gus came by after school, and we went for a walk. I took my basketball, and we ended up shooting hoops at the high school.

"Wonder what's up with your Dad," he said.

"Who knows. Nobody's seen or heard anything. It's not like anyone misses him. Except maybe my Mom."

"She does?" he asked.

"Yeah, I think she does sometimes. She says he used to be different. I say she's better off."

"Women are strange," he said, then pivoted and tried for a three pointer, missing by a mile. There was a hard, angry note in his voice when he said it, and I watched him chase after the ball.

"Soooo . . . ," I said after he'd come back to the court. "How are things going with Cheryl?"

"Oh, alright I guess. She's getting huge, and all puffed out. She can't sleep at night because she says her back hurts. And it seems like all she does is cry all the time. She wants to go to Prom, but the baby's due at the same time. And you can't exactly wear a prom dress when you're nine months pregnant. So, that's been hard for her. Mama says every girl dreams of going to the Prom, but I can't see that it's such a big deal. I mean, it's just another school dance. We've been to plenty of others."

We stopped playing and flopped down on the grass at the edge of the court. "Does your Mama know how to deal with it?" I asked.

"Maybe. But she says I need to learn how myself. Actually she says I don't need to really do anything, just sit there quiet and pretend like I understand. She says men are always wanting to fix things, and women usually just want to be listened to, and that's all. Seems strange to me. When Cher cries it just gets on my nerves."

"Like my Mom missing my Dad—I don't get it."

The light started to fade and grow pale, and we set off toward his house the long way, along the river. "I'm going to be a dad soon," Gus said.

"I know."

"Scares the crap out of me. I've hardly ever even known a real dad."

"There's Mr. Foxworthy. He's kind of like a dad."

"He's old. He hasn't had kids in years. And babies are different than kids anyway. I've never been around babies."

He kept talking. Maybe the cool spring air made him feel like talking. Maybe it was the growing dark. We didn't get many chances to hang out any more. "I guess I'll just take it as it comes," Gus said, throwing the ball spinning up in the air, and catching it with a loud thunk as he talked. "It sure isn't what I planned, my senior year of high school, getting stuck with a kid. But I'm the one who did it, so I'm the one who has to face up."

I didn't have anything to say to that. I was sorry, too. Sorry for all the fun times we could've had together, all the ball games and parties and hanging out we'd already missed. Gus came around when he could, and he was still my best friend, but he usually had to work at the grocery or be with Cheryl.

"I'm never getting married," I said. "I never want kids, either. There's just too many ways to mess it all up."

Gus looked at me and raised his eyebrows. It dawned on me that I wasn't being very encouraging. Of course it was too late for him to think those kinds of thoughts. Not that I could imagine him ever staying single, anyway. Putting Gus all alone in a house would be like putting a straight jacket on a hyperactive monkey, and then stepping back to watch what happened. He'd never last.

"Marriage isn't so bad. You get someone to be with all the time, someone you like. Like a best friend, except you live together, so they're always there. I'm glad I have Cheryl. The last few weeks have been rough, but overall I'm glad. And I can't think having kids will be so bad either, once we get used to it and know what to do. I always thought having a big family would be a blast. There'd always be someone around to hang out with."

"Yeah, you used to say you wished you had ten brothers and sisters. And your Mama would laugh."

"Can you imagine Mama with ten kids? The house all crazy and messed up all the time? She'd go out of her mind."

"But you'd love it."

"Yeah, I probably would."

"She had enough to handle with just you, Gus. You're

probably worth five of the usual kind."

He laughed. He had caused his Mama no small amount of grief over the years, and this past year was enough to beat all the rest. The same thought must have occurred to him, because he sobered up right away.

"Well, my Mama is a good woman. Probably the best woman there ever was. Someday I'm going to have to do something really, really good for her, like buy her a big house or a new car or something, to make up for all the years she had to put up with me."

"Just be a proud papa, and give her a whole pack of grand babies," I said, "and she'll love you till the day she dies. I mean, she'll love you anyway, but I can't think of anything she'd like more than that."

Gus grinned. He was going to be a dad, and no matter what he let on to me or the other kids at school, he was excited about it. He would be a good one, too, I could already see it. He'd always been great around little kids. As usual, I couldn't have been more opposite.

Mom found a place to move into, a two bedroom apartment underneath the Parker's house, another couple from our church. You entered through a door next to the garage, then went down a hallway to the apartment in the back. The living and dining room had a real fireplace, and a big picture window that looked out onto the backyard and Mrs. Parker's rose garden.

Mrs. Kenover was right. People were shy about it at first, maybe not knowing how Mom would react. But pretty soon they started offering to help. Since the furniture we had went with the parsonage, we needed just about everything. But before we could even go shopping we had a kitchen table and four chairs, a sofa bed and a recliner, end tables, a vacuum, and beds enough for all of us. I had to share a room and a bunk bed with Jeremy, but it didn't matter much, since I was leaving for college in a few months.

Mom was able to fix up the apartment the way she liked. The rent was low, so she had enough money left over to buy new curtains and bedspreads and rugs, stuff she'd never bought new before because Father had said things like that were worldly and a waste of God's money. Mrs. Parker went with Mom to the bank and helped her start a bank account, and showed her how to keep track of bills and stuff, because Father had always done all of that. I could tell Mom felt embarrassed, but people seemed happy to step in and help. She started to have more confidence in herself as she learned to do more things.

She also started to make friends with some of the ladies from church. Mom had never had any real friends before except for Mrs. Kenover, and that had probably been an act of charity on Mrs. Kenover's part. But pretty soon it seemed like every time I walked in the door one of the church ladies was there, talking and laughing over coffee or iced tea, bringing a casserole, or helping Mom sew. I think I heard Mom laugh more in those next few months than I had heard in my whole life. And even though I wouldn't wish what had happened to her on anyone, for our family at least, it all seemed for the best in the end.

CHAPTER TWENTY-EIGHT

April 23rd, 1989, on the morning after the Senior Prom, Cheryl had the baby. Gus had called me the afternoon before to tell me Mr. Foxworthy was driving himself, Cheryl and his Mama to the hospital in Lewiston. The baby was born at 4:30 am after a rough night, but I guess that's pretty normal. Gus left a message on our answering machine, which I heard beeping as I walked in the door after a miserable night going to the Prom and pretending to have fun with a bunch of my classmates who were drunk out of their minds. I never got drunk, I didn't like the feeling of being out of control and making a fool of myself. So I generally got stuck being the designated driver for the other guys. I hadn't wanted to go, but Mom said I ought to attend the Prom because that's something everyone should do, and I might regret it if I didn't. The whole night all I could think was, if only she knew. It must have been different when she was young.

On the following day a bunch of us packed into three cars and drove to see Gus and Cher and the baby. We stopped at the IGA and bought a big cake and some balloons and party blowers. Joey Larson gave us a couple of bottles of sparkling cider and a box of cigars, and told me to tell Gus to take the week off.

We walked through the corridors of the hospital, 15 noisy, rowdy high school students riding in on a high from the night before, and were immediately and severely shushed by all the nurses. Looking into the half-open doors of the rooms we passed by I could see people, mostly old people but a few younger ones too, looking helpless and weak in their beds. It gave my stomach a queer feeling, and made me feel half-guilty for being healthy and young. The other kids didn't seem to notice or be bothered by it. Maybe they were used to hospitals. I hadn't been inside a hospital since Jeremy broke his arm when he was two, but that was just the emergency room.

We burst through the door of their room. Poor Cher looked pale and puffy in her hospital gown, without her hair done or any make-up on, but she laughed it off when she saw us and didn't seem to care. She was holding a wrinkly, red baby with a scrunched up face and its body all wrapped up tight like a burrito in a flannel blanket. Gus was sitting at her side bending over it, cooing and shaking a baseball-shaped rattle in its face. Gus took the baby and held it up for all of us to see, and said, "Ladies and Gentlemen, I present to you Adrian Augustine Kenover," and everybody started talking at once. The baby took one look round at the lot of us, and decided to go to sleep.

"Here, Paul—you first," Gus said. "You gotta hold him."

"Me??? I don't . . ." but Gus had already put the thing in my arms. Somebody laughed and snapped a picture, and I looked down. I was surprised how light the baby was. It looked so still and peaceful, I could hardly believe it was real. I started to say, "Does somebody else want to . . ." but before I even finished the sentence one of the girls had snatched him away and settled down in a huddle with all the other females on the far side of the room.

Mrs. Kenover got up from a rocking chair in the corner, where it looked like she'd been taking a nap, and went to the nurses' station to find something to cut the cake with. Gus passed the box of cigars around to all the guys. It all felt surreal, like being caught in a scene from a movie, with everyone saying and doing the exact things you expect them to say and do. In a few months I would be spliced out of the scene. Huge changes loomed ahead of me, and somehow I felt like I'd already stepped onto a different track, moving away from the others. Was already looking back and waving goodbye, but they were all too busy to notice.

I caught Mrs. Kenover watching me, and I went to help her pass out slices of cake. Everyone was laughing and joking now, with Gus and Cheryl in the middle of the group. Gus had his arm around her shoulders, and they looked like they'd been married ten years instead of five months. It was the age-old conversation of 'remember when." Remember this teacher, remember that new girl, remember that night or that summer or that year. Most of us had grown up together, and had gone to the same schools since kindergarten.

There were times that night we laughed so hard we cried.

Periodically, Gus would jump up off the bed to act out something like in the game charades, and that would set us all off. Cheryl told us to stop laughing so much, because it hurt her stomach. Twice the nurses came and asked us to keep it down, then I guess they just gave up. Baby Adrian slept and slept. Mrs. Kenover sat in the corner, rocking him against her chest and just listening, with her eyes closed and a smile on her face. We stayed until a nurse came to take the baby for the night and kicked us all out, saying the new mother needed her sleep. Cheryl protested that she didn't mind having us there at all, but she did look pretty beat.

On the drive home, nobody talked. I looked out the window from the back seat, resting my forehead against the cool glass. Stars pricked the sky like little stabs made by a knife, so beautiful and silent and white it made me ache inside. Between Lewiston and Spring there's just the river, the lonely two-lane highway following its curves, and the mountains and trees climbing up steep on either side. You have to watch out for the deer that sometimes step down onto the road and get transfixed by the headlamps of an oncoming car. There wouldn't be stars like this in Seattle, nor a lonely, empty highway following a river, nor deer. I hadn't thought how much I might miss it all until now.

CHAPTER TWENTY-NINE

On graduation day, Gus and Cheryl walked up to get their diplomas hand in hand, and everybody stood and clapped. First Mrs. Kenover stood, holding baby Adrian, then my mom who was sitting next to her. Then several of the teachers stood up, and after that everyone else followed like a wave. Some of the last people to stand were Cher's parents. Cher's Dad helped his wife up, then put his arm around her strong and tight. From where I was sitting, it looked like there were tears in their eyes. Gus and Cheryl just stood there smiling. Then Gus took off his cap, made a flamboyant bow, and threw his cap out into the audience with a huge whoop.

Summer passed. I was working for another guy from church, nailing shingles onto rooftops and saving money for college. The work was hot and tiring, but it paid well. I came home every night drenched with sweat, showered, ate and fell into bed. The one thought that kept me going was that I was leaving soon. My spirit was restless and my feet itched to travel, and I was ready to leave yesterday.

The day before I left, Gus came over to say goodbye, and we walked to our usual spot by the river. "So, did you make up your mind what you're going to be?" Gus asked.

"I'm thinking about a double major in philosophy and comparative religion."

"And after that?" he asked.

"I don't know. Maybe become a professor or something."

I remember the sunset that night, one of the most incredible things I've ever seen. Streamers of blazing orange began to glow and then spread across the horizon, one after another, until the entire sky looked like a giant, flaming staircase. We sat there and watched it roll itself out like a carpet, and then retreat, step by step, into soft purple dusk. Then the crickets and frogs started up their nightly racket, calling to each other across the river. And I knew that wherever else I went in the world, I would miss this river, these colors, these sounds and sights and smells which had been a part of my life ever since I could remember. And I would miss Gus. What would my life be like without him in it? We'd seen each other almost every day, even if it was just for a few minutes between classes, since I was ten years old.

Gus said, "Boss gave me a promotion last week."

"Yeah?"

"Yeah. Old Mr. Westover is retiring, so I'm going to be the produce manager. They say they've never hired anyone so young to be a manager before, but I've been working hard and they really need somebody, so they're going to give me a chance."

"That's awesome, Gus."

"Yeah. With the increase in salary and the money we've been saving, pretty soon we can get our own little place in town, and give Mama some peace."

He sounded happy and proud. I was proud, too. For a long time, we sat in comfortable silence. Except Gus was drumming a popular song from the radio on his thigh with his fingers. Gus was rarely ever truly silent.

"Do you ever wonder," I asked him, "What if things had been different? I mean, with Adrian and stuff?"

He finished his drumming with a crescendo at the end, letting loose with the final high notes of the song. "Nope, I don't. Mama told me when it happened that there's no use looking back. You have to set your face to what's ahead. And I guess I feel like, with Cheryl and Adrian, I've been blessed, way past what I ever deserved. Cher's a good egg, and Adrian—Adrian is a miracle. You should see Mama with Adrian, Paul. She's happy as a girl." After a minute Gus added, "Besides, what would I have done at college anyway? Probably just drank too much and flunked out, or worse. I'm no scholar, and we both know it. That was Mama's dream, never mine."

It was true. Gus's grades had rarely crept above a C except for maybe P.E., and report cards were always a time of grave disappointment for Mrs. Kenover. If they gave grades for stuff like popularity and the ability to make people laugh, Gus would've been a four point. He was sharp with money and numbers too, as long as he steered clear of abstract stuff like algebra. He'd probably make a good businessman. He might even do better than most of the rest of us, now that he was taking life seriously with his feet on a good track.

Gus went on in his happy-go-lucky way. "If my life is cut out for me from here on out, well, it's not such a bad life. Simple, maybe, but not bad."

I envied him his simplicity, his cheerfulness, his satisfaction. Restlessness stirred in me like the churning of a sea with a storm coming on, and the road ahead looked murky and unclear, full of vague possibilities and dark unknowns. We were so different, Gus and I. Sometimes I wondered how we'd ever been friends at all.

Gus, who despite his simple outlook sometimes seemed to get what I was thinking about even when I couldn't express it, clapped his hand hard on my back. "God's gonna show you the way, Paul. Don't worry. You'll see it."

"I'm not so sure about that."

"He will."

"But how do you know? How do you *know* something like that, so positively?"

"Hey," he said, looking at me, flashing his grin. "Don't ask me such hard questions. I'm no philosophy student. It's me, remember?

The one who doesn't think?"

"I didn't mean that!" I said.

"Yes you did. And it's true. I'm not a complicated guy. But sometimes I do know things. Don't ask me how, I just do. I feel it in my bones, maybe. But God's gonna show you the way. When you really need to know something, there it'll be. I don't want to see you going off to college moping about stuff all the time. Trust me on this one, Paul. Lighten up a bit. Be sure and go out with the guys on the weekends, and have a beer once in a while. And try smiling more. Here I am, your best friend, come to say goodbye. I hate to leave you looking like such a dope."

Married or not, he was the same Gus as ever. Never satisfied till he left you with a laugh.

"Hey, I love you man," he said. "Don't ever forget it. And don't you dare go off to Seattle and never back come home to visit. Mama and I would never forgive you."

He hugged me hard, slapping his palm against my back, and I hugged back. For a few minutes, neither one of us could talk. Then we stepped back and shook hands.

As he jogged back toward his place, Gus turned and called out, "Hey, Cheryl's going to send you care packages of homemade cookies every month. I'll superintend and make sure that she does. And pictures of Adrian—tons and tons of pictures!"

"My album's gonna be packed by the time I'm through with

school with pictures of you and your ten kids!" I yelled back.

"You know it, man. You know it!"

I watched him jog away, until his white t-shirted back faded into the dimming evening light. Then, with a lump like a rock stuck down in my throat, I shoved my hands into my pockets and walked toward home, toward suitcases and boxes and the University of Washington in Seattle, where one of Mom's new friends from church would drive us all early the next morning.

All that summer I couldn't wait to ditch our small town and move to the city. But when the last night comes and it's time to say goodbye, maybe you can't help but think a little like Dorothy that there's no place like home, and no people like the people you knew growing up. Even back then, as a just-graduated high school student who was thrashing to get away, I thought about these things. No matter where else life took me, my roots were sunk deep in the hard, pine-needle littered ground right next to a turquoise and white metal trailer perched on the edge of a schoolyard, shadowed all around by the mountains and trees.

That night I thought about my Mom, who was doing pretty well now in spite of everything, learning to smile again after years and years when she'd forgotten how. And I wondered as I sometimes did about my Dad—where he was living, and whether or not he ever thought about us, or if he had just stuck us up high on a shelf out of sight and moved on. I thought about Jeremy, who had stopped picking on other kids at school but still didn't have any friends, and I thought about Gus and Cheryl and Adrian, loving each other and sticking together even when life wasn't what they'd expected. And at the base of all of these things, at the place where the tree divided and all the branches spread out, was Mrs. Kenover— never wanting to step into the foreground, but present, always, in the background, thinking about other people's needs and putting aside her own. Sometimes she was so quiet you could forget she was even there. But somehow, when she was there, she affected everything.

CHAPTER THIRTY

It was midway through my freshman year at University of Washington, during the week before finals—Dead Week. I was in my dorm room, sleeping late on a Saturday morning, when one of the guys from down the hall banged on my door, yelling that there was someone downstairs to see me.

"Just a minute, I'm coming," I said, pulling on jeans, a sweatshirt, and a baseball cap. "Who is it?" I asked as I opened the door.

"I dunno," he said, "just some old guy asking for you. I told him I didn't think you were up yet, but he said he'd wait."

"Alright, I'll go down," I said, walking over to the sink to brush my teeth and splash some water on my face. Whoever it was, I hoped he wouldn't take long. It was eleven o'clock already, and I had a paper due Monday for Western Civ that I hadn't even started. I pounded down the three flights of stairs into the lobby. Then I saw him, and I stopped short.

It was my Dad. At first, I didn't even recognize him. Then when I did, it was a shock. He'd lost maybe twenty pounds, and his hair was thin and dull looking. His clothes hung on him, and they weren't his clothes—at least not like any clothes that I remembered. I'd rarely seen my father without a button-down shirt and slacks. Now he wore a baggy pair of cargo pants, a flannel shirt, work boots, and an old coat that looked like it came from a thrift shop. He was pacing back and forth, looking nervously out the windows at all the students walking up and down the street. And I remembered that he had always paced. Impatient and demanding, he would walk back and forth across the kitchen floor as he shot out orders for the day, usually to my Mom. I stood there and studied him for a few minutes, my mind reeling with conflicting thoughts and emotions. I felt curiosity, and a sudden kind of grief that hit me like a punch in the gut. But most of all, I felt anger. Let him make the first move, I thought. I sure as hell wasn't going to. My mouth felt dry as lint, and my heart started pounding beneath my sweatshirt so loudly I thought everyone around must be able to hear.

At last he saw me. He took a few strides forward, then hesitated and stopped, looking at me. His face looked like the face of a haggard old bird, sharp and hungry somehow. Then he started toward me again, and I looked away.

"Paul," he said, then he shoved his hands in his pockets, and looked down at the floor. But I had seen that his hands were shaking. I didn't know what to say. What did he expect me to say?

"Can I take you out for coffee somewhere?"

"Yeah, I guess," I answered.

We walked out to the car without speaking, the same old blue Oldsmobile he'd had for years. We drove in silence until he pulled into an IHOP nearby. After a girl led us to a booth and we both sat down, I said, "Do you mind if I order some food? I just got up."

"No, go right ahead. Order whatever you want."

So I got the full-blown special for $9.95—pancakes, hash browns and eggs, bacon and sausage, the works—along with a coffee and a fresh squeezed orange juice. Who knew if I'd ever see him again, and I figured he owed me that much at least. He ordered himself a cup of black coffee.

While we were waiting for the food to come, he asked the usual kinds of questions. How were my classes going, how did I like Seattle, how were Gus and the baby. How was Jeremy, and was he still having trouble in school?

"Jeremy's doing great," I said. "Gus kind of took him under his wing this summer. He buys him flight magazines and stuff, and even took him to the air show up in Spokane. So he's started studying like crazy, hoping to get an air force scholarship. He still doesn't have any friends, but at least he's not getting into trouble."

I emphasized my words, making it all sound as positive and cheerful as I could. Gus was acting like the dad you should be, I thought. I wanted it to hurt. But my dad just smiled a little and said he was glad to hear it. Then he said, "I imagine Mrs. Kenover's been a real help to your mom."

"Oh yeah, more than anyone," I said. "You know her."

Dad nodded, then looked off and out the window. "Yes, I guess I finally do," he said. I didn't quite get that, but just then the waitress came with our food, and asked if we needed anything else. I shook my head no. It looked, and smelled, absolutely heavenly to me. The potatoes were crisp and brown, the eggs quivering just so, the sausage and bacon sizzling, and the pancakes were an even golden color. It had been a long time since I'd had a breakfast like that.

As soon as we'd finished the obligatory prayer-before-meals and before I'd even taken a bite, Dad blurted out a small speech. "Paul, I . . . I was wrong. I made a lot of foolish mistakes. I wanted to find you to say I'm sorry. And I hope that someday, you can find it in your heart to forgive me."

I was so surprised I dropped my fork. Never on this earth, never in my entire memory, had I ever heard my Dad say he was sorry. It was the last thing I'd expected, and it floored me. And he actually looked me in the eye when he said it. When he had finished, he looked desperately out the window, around the restaurant, and finally down at the napkin he was twisting in his hands. Then he put the napkin down, carefully folded it in half and smoothed it flat. His hands were shaking again. This time, he didn't even try to hide them.

I sat there for a few minutes, my breakfast forgotten. I wanted to be angry at him. I wanted to say something mean, to pay him out for all the years he had made us miserable, with his self-righteousness and his yelling, with his total obliviousness to anyone else's needs but his own. But looking at him then, I just couldn't. He looked so worn down and miserable, so thin, and nervous as hell. He looked like a man who had been dragged through the worst, and maybe come up out of the muck, but just barely. He looked so different than I'd ever expected.

I suddenly knew then, and I believe still, that when a person is already covered in shame, it's only meanness that could dig in with a shovel and heap more dirt on his head. So I swallowed hard. Swallowed down all my anger, and all the mean things I wanted to say and said, "Yeah, Dad. I think I can forgive you."

He let out a sigh, flashed a near-smile in my direction, then grabbed his coffee cup and turned his head real quick to look out the window again, blinking hard. Jesus, it looked like he was going to cry. Then he said, measuring each word carefully, "That's good. That's more than I could have expected. I'm glad."

I waved down the waitress to get another fork, then tucked in. He didn't talk for a while, just sipped his coffee and looked out the window at the cars passing by. At last, as I started on my pancakes, he looked at me directly and said, "Paul, how is your Mother? Is she all right?"

In his eyes there was an intensity that took me off guard. I could almost feel him sweating and holding his breath, waiting for my answer. I realized this was probably the real reason for him coming to find me, to ask about her. Not that it canceled out all the rest. I guess it would be natural for him to think of her first.

"She's doing great," I said cautiously. "She found a place for us to live and fixed it all up, painting and sewing curtains and all that. In that apartment below the Parker's house. She got a job with Mr. Oldham, you know the lawyer from church. And she's made a lot of friends."

"Does she have enough money?" he asked, still looking intent at me.

"I think she's doing OK. The Parkers don't charge us much rent, and thankfully I made good money last summer roofing, and got scholarships that pay for most of my school. And yeah, she's happy," I said, looking him in the eye. What the hell, I thought—I may as well be honest. "In fact, she's happier than she's been in years."

To my surprise, my Dad sat back against the seat with what looked like relief, and didn't flinch or grimace one bit. He just said, "I'm glad to hear she's doing well." Then his tight, nervous face seemed to fall slack, and he just looked tired and sad. He stared out the window again, his hands wrapped around his coffee mug, and didn't speak another word as I finished the last of my breakfast and juice. I didn't usually make it up in time to eat before classes, and this beat cafeteria food any day. I hoped he had the money to pay for it; he didn't look too well off. I asked, "What are you doing now, Dad? I mean, for a job and stuff?"

He jumped when I spoke. "Oh, odd jobs. This and that," he

said.

"Where are you living?"

"I've got an apartment in Spokane. Close to the downtown."

"I guess," I said, knowing it was awkward but not knowing what else to say, "You won't go back to preaching again."

"No, I should think not," he said, with a bitter, short laugh. It made me feel sorrier for him than ever. He added, so softly I almost couldn't hear, "No, Son, I think God's through with me in that department. I'm not much use to him now."

I didn't know what to say after that. It sounded off, to say that about God. But I'd abandoned reading the Bible years ago, so what did I know. I drained the last of my coffee. Looking embarrassed, he looked up at me and asked, "Just one more question. Your mother—is she seeing anyone?"

"You mean like, a man?"

"Well, yes."

"Of course not," I said. "I think . . ." I began, and then I wasn't sure if I should continue, or how. It seemed like an awful can of worms. Who was I to open it? All I knew was, this was a different man than the man I'd known before, and this man ought to know. And maybe, there wouldn't be another chance. So I decided to tell him. "Mom told me how she loved you in the beginning, how you were happy together. She told me that on the day you left. I think . . .

I think she still loves you. Even though I don't see why."

Dad stared at me like a fish, unblinking, uncomprehending. Then he looked down into his cup, shaking his head. "No, no, it's too late for me, Son. Your Mom deserves someone better than me." He turned and looked out the window again, his body slumped over like a deflated balloon. I've never seen a face so bleak and sad, before or since. It seemed then like he was past tears, past hope, past the reach of anyone or anything. I sat there in the heavy, loaded silence, not knowing what to do or say. Then he sat up abruptly and said, "I'm ready to go."

He flagged down the waitress for the check. He handed her a twenty, telling her to keep the change, and then we got up and walked out to the car. I made a few attempts at conversation but he didn't answer, and within minutes we were back at my dorm. I said bye and reached over to open the car door when he caught my arm and asked me if I could do a favor for him. I answered sure, and he handed me an envelope and asked if I could give it to my Mom. I looked inside, and there were six crisp one hundred dollar bills inside. "I'd like to help her out with expenses, when I can," he said.

"I can give it to her next week, when I go home for break," I answered. He said he would appreciate it, and I shut the door. And then he drove away.

When I first handed my Mom the envelope and said I'd seen my Dad, she turned white, bit her lip, and gripped the nearby counter to steady herself as if she would keel over in a faint. Then she grilled me about every detail of that meeting. She wanted to know what he had looked like and sounded like, what he was wearing, where he was living and working—everything. I realized how dumb I had been not to ask more questions, because I didn't have many answers to give. The way she started jumping around the kitchen like the mad hatter that afternoon, talking faster and faster as she cooked dinner and went from one thing to the next, I should have guessed she wouldn't rest until she had found out more.

On Christmas Eve, the three of us went out for dinner with some of Dad's money. The rest Mom put into a savings account. On Christmas day we went to Mrs. Kenover's trailer along with Gus and Cheryl and baby Adrian, who was crawling all over and getting into everything. I kept watching Mom to see if she would say that Dad had made contact with us again, but she was quiet all evening. With Gus and Cheryl and the baby, there was enough craziness to keep us all entertained. The whole party came to a panicked halt at one point when Adrian started choking and turning blue after trying to eat a big wad of wrapping paper.

Mrs. Kenover made turkey and mashed potatoes and homemade rolls, green beans and my favorite, Jell-o made with 7 up and applesauce. It was like her to remember. There was pecan pie and apple pie for dessert, served up with real whipped cream. I had a big slice of each, and thought about I would soon be going back to dorm food, supplemented with ramen noodles and fifty-nine cent bean burritos. After dinner, we turned out all the lights except the fat multicolored bulbs on the tree, and sang Christmas carols. It was one of those perfect evenings when you wish you could hit pause, and make it last forever. I guess you never outgrow the spell of a lit-up Christmas tree in a dark room.

Mrs. Kenover had a rich, deep voice, and I loved to hear her sing. She knew all the verses to the carols, and sometimes ended up finishing them solo while the rest of us sat and listened. I was glad she didn't get embarrassed and stop. Gus had a good voice too, kind of a high, smooth tenor, and he even knew how to do harmony on some of the songs. Even baby Adrian stayed quiet. I looked over at Mom as we sang. Her head was leaning back, and her eyes were closed. She wasn't singing with the rest of us, but just sitting there quiet and peaceful with her hands in her lap, like she used to do sometimes when I was a kid, resting her head on that same green sofa. I wondered if she was praying, and if so, what she was praying for. Ever since her first flurry of questions, she'd been quiet as a clam. She didn't want to talk about it, but she'd been distracted and far away, and I was sure she'd thought of little else but my Dad since I'd handed her that envelope.

I know now that she was indeed praying that night, and that she wanted my Dad to come back, but she was afraid. Things had been bad for her for years. She'd watched her husband change from an earnest young man fresh out of Seminary who she'd loved and who made her laugh, into a self-righteous, anger driven monster that she feared and endured. Even though it seemed like Dad might have changed, things were pretty good for her by then. She'd started to make a life for herself. Months later I thought, why would she want to walk away from that, from the only peace and good she'd had for years? Throw it all away on a man who had done nothing but hurt her over and over again?

How can you explain love like that? Love that no matter what happens, doesn't give up? I watched my Mom during those few weeks I had off from school. She kept quiet on the outside, but underneath her resolution grew. I couldn't understand it. If I had been her, I would have washed my hands of the whole thing years before, would have cut my losses and left. So on the night before I left, when she asked for my help to find out where my Dad was living, I wasn't exactly surprised. And I promised I would help her.

CHAPTER THIRTY-ONE

With mixed feelings to say the least, I lifted my fist and knocked on the thin door with its peeling brown paint. After a moment I heard steps advancing from the inside. The apartment building was located on Ash Street, a busy arterial through a depressing neighborhood just north of downtown Spokane. But at least it was easy to find. My father opened the door.

"Paul," he said, and stood there staring stupidly at me.

"Can I come in?" I asked. It was the middle of March, and the wind was biting and cold.

"Yes, of course," he said, and he stepped back, holding the door open wide.

He waited wordless while I took off my coat and looked around. It was a small, dark apartment on the first floor, with puke green carpet and dingy, smoke-stained walls. From the entryway I could see in to the single bedroom to my left. The bathroom was straight ahead, and to my right was the living room with a beat up old couch and chair, and a small dining table pushed against the far wall. The kitchen must have been in the back, through the open doorway in the far corner. There was a bowl of soup on the table with a glass of milk alongside it, and a book lying face down beside.

"I was just sitting down for dinner. Would you like me to make you some?" he said.

"Are you sure you don't mind?" I asked. I had driven down from Seattle and hadn't eaten anything since grabbing a candy bar at the gas station halfway.

"No. It's quick to make."

I peeked into the bowl and saw the familiar squiggles of ramen noodles, mixed with previously frozen peas. "I know," I said. "It's a favorite on campus. Ten cents a pack."

I followed him into the kitchen and watched as he rinsed the pan, measured out the water, and put it on the burner to boil. Every movement seemed measured and slow. His voice when he spoke was lifeless and flat, with any expression his face might reveal held carefully in.

"So, how did you find me?" he asked.

"The financial aid office. I told them I was your son, and I needed money for next semester's bill."

He looked up and asked sincerely, "Do you need money?"

"No, I'm fine. That was just the excuse I gave them."

"Hmph," he said, looking down to rip open the flavor packet, stir it into the boiling soup, and pour it all into a bowl. My little white lie probably got his goat. He was always a stickler for the truth.

He brought the bowl to the table, then poured a second glass of milk and brought that too, and we sat down. He bowed his head for a quick, silent prayer, while I sat and watched him. I couldn't get over the outward changes in him. This was my father sitting next to me, but it just wouldn't sink in. He looked like he'd aged a million miles and twenty years. We started to eat.

"Actually," I said, trying to sound casual, "It was Mom that asked me to find you."

"She knows where I am?" he asked, looking up, panic stricken.

"No, not yet. I promised her I'd try and find you, but I thought I'd check things out myself first. Mom wanted me to say thank you for the money."

Since Christmas he had sent an envelope around the first of every month, with three crisp one hundred dollar bills folded up inside a blank piece of typing paper and placed in a business sized envelope. They were postmarked from the main post office in downtown Spokane, but there was no return address.

He waved his hand at my words. "The money is nothing," he

said.

"Well, she said to say it anyway. Dad . . ." I started. He stopped his spoon midway to his mouth, then lowered it back down into his soup bowl and looked at me. "What happened to you? I mean, how did you end up here?"

He ate another mouthful, and set his spoon down precisely to the right of his bowl. Then he leaned back in his chair with his arms folded against his chest, looking down. He was quiet for a long time.

"Son, I . . ." he started. Then he looked at me skeptically. "Are you sure you want to hear all this?"

"Yeah I want to hear it. I'm your son, aren't I? And you just seem so different."

He looked out the living room window with its curtains open to the street, arms still folded across his chest. At the headlights and tail lights of the cars and trucks speeding past, and the noise of engines and wheels and brakes of the six o'clock commute in the early Spring dark. Then, still looking down at the table, he started to talk.

"Son, when I look back on those months before I left you and your Mom . . . ," and then he shook his head. "No, not months, years —I may as well begin at the beginning. It was a long, slow fall for me. It all started with my pride. I thought I was God's chosen man. I was going to build his church, and it was going to be spotless and pure. I was doing it all for him, it was all for the glory of God—at least that's what I told myself at the time. I poured my life into my work. There wasn't anything—not my wife, not my children, that could be held up next to doing God's work. Your poor mother. She swallowed it all whole, and tried to support me the best she could. She was willing to give up everything, too. Both of us were pumped up full of foolish ideals, in the beginning." He paused, shaking his head again.

"So, we arrived in Spring, fresh out of Seminary. But I was mistaken about some important things," he said, looking up at me. "A husband and wife shouldn't have to choose between love for each other and love for God. The two things shouldn't be pitted against each other like that. I learned that too late, after I'd already made a mess of everything. But enough of that now, I'll get back to the story. First Baptist in Spring was my first church, and I was going to show the world that I could make a success of it. But the tighter I held on to my ideals, the more I tried to move forward with my plans, the more it all seemed to slip away. The people wouldn't get on board, wouldn't trust me, and rejected every new idea I put forward. The pastor who had been at the church before I arrived, Reverend Baxter, had been there for thirty years. Everyone loved him, and no matter what I did, it didn't measure up. All of them, even the best of them, would say, 'Reverend Baxter would do it this way,' or 'Reverend Baxter always said such and such.' It drove me wild, and I felt more determined than ever that I would show them."

"Then some things happened early on, when Mrs. Kenover first arrived in town. She got off the bus that first night and, finding the door unlocked, slept in the church. I heard about it early the next morning—Boy, did I ever hear about it, with a nasty anonymous phone call, and a note slipped under the door of my office filled with the worst kind of small-town, small-minded gossip that spreads like wildfire in a closed-up little place like Spring. So the next day, I went in early to surprise the girl and take control of the situation. I talked down to her, and threatened to send her home. And the way she looked at me that day—she didn't say a word—but the way she looked at me made me feel ten inches tall. Maybe you can imagine, Son, you know her. She's a great woman, but she can be awfully dignified when she wants to be. I don't think she tries to intimidate others, but you know what I mean."

I nodded. It wasn't hard to picture.

"Well, I couldn't tolerate that. At least at the time I didn't think I could. I was the Pastor of the church, and I was going to show this teenage girl who was in charge. I had some wrong ideas about black people back then, and I had assumed the worst about her, thinking she was an immoral woman, some kind of trouble maker. Well then . . . I'm sorry this is taking so long," he interrupted himself, looking up at me. "Do you have somewhere else you need to be tonight?"

"No, no, I'm fine. Keep going. I want to hear it," I said. I'd pieced together some stuff from bits and pieces I'd heard over the years, but I'd never heard the story whole like this.

"Well then, thankfully for Mrs. Kenover, the Foxworthys stepped up and took her in. And I thought I could forget about the whole thing. But she came to church with the Foxworthy's and sat there in the pew, week after week. And people kept whispering. There were rumors insinuating that I had been in a secret relationship with the girl, and that was the reason she came to our town. She was pregnant and nobody knew the father, and there are people in the world who seem to thrive on that kind of intrigue. I kept getting anonymous letters and phone calls, filthy things. Instead of sharing the situation with your Mother and standing together in it, I thought I had to shield her from it all, and I was trying to bear it all alone. But more and more the pressure built up, until the situation became intolerable, and I felt I had to take some kind of stand, and make it clear to others that the whole thing had nothing to do with me."

"So, one Sunday in an attempt to address the situation I gave a sermon, effectively putting Mrs. Kenover to shame in front of the whole congregation. I thought I was standing against immorality. After all, *she* was the runaway teen who had gotten herself pregnant. And as I said, I had some mistaken, mistaken ideas about black people back then. I was repeating things that I'd been taught in seminary and read in books, but the truth was I'd never met a real live black person to actually talk to. I was just picking up bits I'd heard and patching them together in my own defense. I thought I was standing up for righteousness, and the holiness of God. I was going to come down hard on gossip, too, that Sunday, but I never got that far. The Foxworthys got up and left at the beginning of the sermon, taking the girl with them. And I never regained control of the room after that."

"All that time I kept trying to push Mrs. Kenover and her problems away from me. But I was absolutely in the wrong, Son, and I think even at the time I knew it. I should have been reaching out to help, not pushing her away. Even then, I knew the girl had probably been raped. I don't think anyone ever got the full story out of her, but she had indicated as much on the morning I first met her and tried to send her home. But back then, I thought of her as my tormentor. I even wondered if she might be the source of the rumors and the anonymous letters—they had certainly started on the day she arrived. I thought if I could just get rid of her, if she would just go to some other town, my problems would be solved. Maybe that sounds crazy to you, but that's what I was thinking at the time."

Actually, it made a lot of sense to me. Suddenly, a whole slew of things I'd never understood—things unmentionable and things unsaid, underlying tensions, and comments made by people in town, kind of fell into place. I realized after a minute that my Dad had stopped talking and was watching me, waiting for some reaction or response. "Go on," I said.

"Following that Sunday, I lost half my church body because of what I'd done. The Foxworthys left, and took the best of my congregation with them. The Foxworthys went to the Catholics, which I simply couldn't believe at the time. A few tried to start a little church of their own, which floundered and eventually died. But most just drove twenty miles up the river to the next closest Baptist church. I was devastated, and I began to realize how wrongly I'd handled everything. But I wouldn't admit that to anyone else. I kept losing ground, but I didn't know how to turn around and go back. Instead I became more determined than ever. I would make a success of that church, or I would die trying. And I decided nobody —not the Foxworthys, not my wife, and certainly not some Negro teenager from who knows where, was going to stand in my way. That was the extent of my pride, Son. That was the only thing I could see."

Dad paused then, and drank the rest of his milk. Then he looked down at the table again and continued. "Years went by. I spent more time on my sermons, went to more meetings, and made sure I had control of everything that went on in that little church, and just about every word that was said. And the church kept going. It wasn't the glorious thing I'd dreamed it would be, but it kept going. Lord knows how or why it didn't sink. Half the congregation was afraid of me, and the other half simply couldn't imagine being anything but Baptist, and didn't want to make the long drive every Sunday down the river. A few of them actually approved of how I'd handled the situation with Mrs. Kenover—the last ones I should have listened to in the first place. They only went on to cause more problems. And so for a long time I fooled myself that I was doing well, and that God himself approved of me."

"Then I found out somehow that you boys and your Mom were going over to the Kenover woman's trailer. Your Mom didn't tell me; she knew how I'd feel about it. But in any case I found out. And I tried to forbid her from going, to make her stop. But that's when your Mom gave me the surprise of my life, and she said no. She just put her foot down and said no to me. She'd never done that before. She insisted that you, Paul, had made a good friend in Gus, and that you needed that friendship. She said that Gus was the first real friend you'd ever had, and that it was important for a boy to have friends. We fought about it late one night when you boys were asleep. I was so angry with her, suddenly all I could see was white. I lost control that night, and I hit your mother. I hit her so hard she fell unconscious on the floor. I was afraid at first that I had killed her, and I started crying and praying to God that she would get up. Then I saw her start to sit up, and she was crying, too. And then I ran. I got in the car and I just drove."

"I was horrified at what I'd done. Me, a minister of the gospel —I had lost control and hit my wife. What would I do next? I loved your Mom, Paul. Despite everything, and no matter what it looked like from the outside, I've always loved your Mom. I know I didn't show it very well, and I certainly didn't treat her like she deserved." Dad's voice had become high pitched and tight, and two blotches of hot pink were showing high up on his cheekbones. He squeezed his eyes shut and was quiet for a minute, clenching his jaw, fighting for control.

"From that point on I was afraid. I could never trust myself again. When I felt that kind of anger coming on, when I knew I was coming close to losing control, I would run. I'd leave the house, go on a drive, or lock myself in my study. And after that, too, I felt like I'd lost your Mom. Maybe she had loved me once, but after what I'd done, how could she ever trust me again? And she had defied me over the black women. I blamed Mrs. Kenover more than ever. I hated it when you all went over there, but I let it be. I remember being afraid of what Mrs. Kenover would say to you, afraid she would turn you all against me. I know her better now."

He paused again, and I waited. I knew there was more to come. It was a long story, and I could tell it was taking a lot out of him to tell it.

"The years went by, and things went from bad to worse. My anger only got worse. I couldn't trust myself around you boys or your Mom. The only way I felt I could keep going was to escape. I escaped into my study, into my books. Sometimes I just got in the car and drove. And then later there was Miss Briggs. She never meant anything to me. She was a distraction, nothing more. You can believe me or not, Paul, but I never slept with the woman. She flirted with me, teased me, made things feel a bit lighter. Had it gone on it might have become more, but thankfully you put a stop to all that," he said, looking up at me. "When I left I tried to convince her to come with me, but she didn't want to. I don't know what became of her after that. She had family in Missoula, so maybe she went back home."

"So then I was alone. I had no money, no family, no job. I'd been caught red-handed, and shown to be a fraud. I was nothing. I drove around for a few days, trying to figure out what to do, and ended up here in Spokane. I couldn't find work, not even pumping gas. Nobody wanted an ex-preacher from a little town in Idaho. I was sleeping in my car, in parking lots and on neighborhood streets.

Sometimes a patrol car would drive up and tell me to move. I had to scrounge in garbage bins for food, and find a different place to sleep every night. It looked like the end for me. I just couldn't see any place I could go."

"One day I was sitting on a bench in the big park downtown. I was ready to call it quits. I thought about driving the car off the edge of the road into the river. I'd made a mess of my life, and I didn't see any way out. And then a black man came and sat next to me. A black man. After all the things I'd said and done."

At this point he started tearing up. I waited, staring down at the table, taking it all in. Half afraid to move, lest I break the spell and he stopped talked. He got up to find a tissue, and blew his nose. It took him a few minutes before he was able to continue.

"And I thought, God, this is you humbling me. After all my mistakes, here you come to rub my nose in it. But the man was kind, Paul. He was so kind. He was a Minister who worked at the mission down on the corner. On the day he found me, I was dizzy and weak from eating almost nothing for several days. He put his arm around me and walked me to the mission, then sat me down with a hot meal. I got a shower, some fresh clothes, and a good, clean bed for the night. The man didn't ask anything in return, and he didn't ask any questions, at least not at first. Later I told him some of the things I'd said and done, so he'd know what kind of man he was helping. But he was just as kind after that."

Dad had broken down again, and was really crying.

Fascinated, I watched him. I'd never seen him cry before. It made me feel strange inside, like the world was tipping somehow, like all the things I thought I knew and felt sure of, suddenly seemed unsure and surreal. At last he seemed to be done. He blew his nose again and continued.

"So I worked there at the mission, helping serve food and wash dishes, mopping the floor and making beds and just doing anything else that needed done. When they heard I'd been a pastor they asked me if I'd like to take a turn preaching after mealtimes, but I said no. That was OK with them, they didn't push. I did agree to go visit at the jail. I do that Saturday mornings now. The mission puts on a small service there, and I help with that."

"In time they helped me find a job, and helped set me up here in my own apartment. They helped find the furniture too. I work for a construction company on a framing crew. I started with doing simple clean up around the job site, picking up wood scraps and things. Now the foreman is training me to do some measuring and cutting, and giving me simple jobs to do. I got a raise, and the boss says if I do well, he'll give me another raise and more training this summer. So far it seems to be working out all right."

He stopped then, and looked down at his hands. They were rough hands now, no longer smooth and white, but reddened by sun and wind, with thick calluses on the palms. Then he folded his hands together and put them in his lap, looked at me and said nervously, "So that's the whole story. I can't imagine what you think of it all, knowing the truth about your father."

I couldn't imagine, either. In fact, I couldn't think of a single thing to say. The two of us sat there at the table for five minutes or more, me just trying to digest it all, and him nervously clasping and unclasping his hands and looking out the window with his cold ramen noodles sitting uneaten in front of him. The noises in the room seemed to grow louder—the ticking of the clock on the wall, the faint electric sound of the baseboard heater, and the cars on the street outside, not as busy now, but still a steady hum. I realized how weary I felt. The past week of papers and exams and late nights out with friends seemed to all crash down on me at once. At last I said, "Is it OK if I camp here tonight? I can head home in the morning. I got up early, and I think I'm too tired to drive the rest of the way tonight."

"Of course. The sofa isn't the most comfortable, but it's yours if you want it."

"Thanks," I said. Dad found me a blanket, then went into the kitchen to do the dishes and wipe up. My mind was spinning, and I was too tired to think, too tired even to take off my shoes or jeans. I grabbed a couch pillow, pulled the blanket up over me, and must have dropped off to sleep before he even finished. When I woke up the sun was high in the sky and he was already gone, probably to visit the prisoners. I folded the blanket neatly on the couch and left. I stopped at McDonald's on the way out of town for breakfast and then drove the rest of the way home, thinking about all the things Dad had told me. And about how different the world was, and our family was, than I ever would have expected when I was growing up.

CHAPTER THIRTY-TWO

I told my Mom about the visit, and how Dad had ended up homeless on the street, but was now working on a construction crew and living in an apartment. She was very quiet for the rest of the week. Whatever she was thinking about it all, she didn't share it with me. I was out most of the time hanging out with friends anyway. Soon after I left, she sent him a letter. About a month later, she went up to visit him. I offered to meet her there, but she wanted to go by herself. After that she started going up about once a month, and they went to see a counselor. Eventually, after Jeremy graduated and left for the Air Force, Mom gave up her job and the basement apartment, and moved back in with Dad in Spokane. They didn't remarry, but then they had never divorced. They just had a several-year intermission.

I visited a few times a year if I wasn't traveling, once for Thanksgiving or Christmas, and once again in the summer. It was like they had built a little house: The walls were constructed of memories and pain and all that they had endured, but inside there was a kind of peace and love. For anyone outside those walls, it felt awkward and off limits. It just wasn't a place others could enter in, not even me as their son. They would listen to me talk. They were interested in my life and in what I was thinking about. But I could never seem to really connect. Too much water under the bridge, maybe. Too much stuff had happened. They seemed happy enough as a couple—sometimes they held hands when they walked, or sat next to each other on the couch, Dad with his arm around Mom. I'd never once seen them doing that when I was growing up. But we had never been happy all together as a family. I'm not sure what I expected when they got back together. Maybe it was just too late.

Mom and Dad settled in Spokane and eventually bought a little house on the north side. Mom found another job at a law office and learned to garden and grow flowers, and Dad helped her dig and plant stuff outside. He had become muscled and brown from working in the sun. They attended church regularly, and Dad volunteered at the Mission. Jeremy never visited at all. He'd made it on to some kind of elite Special Ops unit in the Air Force, and he was stationed all over the world. Most of the time we weren't even allowed to know where he was. On the few occasions when I talked to him, I got the impression he liked it that way. He was my only brother, but it felt like I'd never really known him at all.

As for me, I went on for my doctorate in British Columbia, then settled into teaching and academic life as a Professor of Comparative Religion at Portland State University. I liked the buzz of Portland—my apartment in a lively downtown neighborhood, the ethnic restaurants and the many colored faces, and the anonymity and distractions of a big city. But deep down, I felt rootless and confused. More than anything I loved to travel, and my job gave me an excuse to visit all kinds of places, with their temples and shrines and mosques. I had a series of girlfriends, but nothing serious. I could never seem to let anyone get that close. After a few months, I would start to feel cagey and irritable, and break things off.

I believed in some kind of god, I knew that much. I spent my days studying and lecturing on the topic. But what kind? What kind of god would let my Mom go through the things she did, or allow the kind of stuff that happened to Mrs. Kenover, not to mention the worse varieties of suffering that happen every day all over the world. It always seemed to circle back around to that for me. And despite all my traveling and study, I still didn't have a good answer. Religious faith has inspired some the most beautiful art and architecture and poetry known to man. But pick up the rock and look underneath, and some of the most hideous and horrible things men and women have done to each other have also been done in the name of god. The question that drove me to keep reading and writing was this: Why the draw and pull of religion? In every human culture, some form of worship has existed. Those cultures that try to suppress it only push it underground, it never really dies. Why couldn't we just walk away from it? Why couldn't I?

Gus worked his way up in the grocery business, and in his early thirties he bought the local hardware and auto parts store. By his early forties he owned several small stores along the river, from

Lewiston all the way across the state into Montana, and up north into Coeur d'Alene. He was a smart businessman and thrived on being hyper-involved in the community. From being active in his parish to serving on the school board, you name it, he was in the thick of it. Most years I made it down to meet him in Spring, or sometimes at a campground if it was summer, and spent a few days hanging out with his family. He and Cheryl ended up having five kids. Being with their family was wild and crazy and totally Gus, a 180 degree turn from the quiet and reserve at my parent's house. They never sat down except to eat or maybe watch a movie or play a video game—it was go, go, go and active all the time. I could only take a few days of it at a time, but ironically I felt happier and more rooted there than anywhere else. Mrs. Kenover stayed on in her little trailer, but she was often there at Gus's place, and always available to share a cup of coffee, a listening ear, and her steady, wise perspective on things if you asked. It's a good thing in life to have old friends—people who've known me through all the stuff that's happened. People that, when I'm with them, I don't have to try and explain. I can let stuff go, and just be. Gus and his household provided a definite break from the competitive, one-upmanship and back-biting of academic life, and the so-called friendships therein. So I tried to make it down at least once a year.

Part Five: Gus

CHAPTER THIRTY-THREE

It was Thanksgiving weekend, 2012 when we found out Mama had cancer. It had started in her breast and then spread into her lungs. She'd been having pain in her shoulder and chest for months, but Mama being Mama, she didn't tell anyone until we found out for ourselves after she collapsed at the sink, doing dishes after cooking a huge meal. I sent her to the best specialists in Spokane, a city chock-full of hospitals and a regional medical center for all the surrounding area and up into Canada. But the doctors said the cancer had already spread too far. There was nothing they could do except try and make her comfortable until the end.

When the doctor told Mama, I was with her in the hospital room. She looked small and thin, shrunk back into herself in her hospital gown on the upraised bed. She didn't say a word, but just sat there nodding with her eyes closed, looking tired. I was the one who did all the talking. I told the doctor that if there was anything, *anything* I could do to save Mama, I would do it. I would fly her halfway across the world. I would quit my job and sell the stores. I kept at him, until at last he apologized abruptly and left the room.

Mama told me to cool myself down. She said she was ready to go anytime Jesus called for her. "I'll miss the babies though," she said, looking down at her hands and turning them over in her lap, looking first at the worn tops, then her pink palms, then the tops again. By that time we'd had our youngest, little Alise. We also had Adrian, Alex, Ariel, and Ashley. "It would be nice to see all the babies grow up, and make their way into the world."

Me, I was anything but ready to let her go. I was devastated. And I was fighting mad. I couldn't imagine life without Mama there in the background, rooting for me. Always telling me the hard stuff I didn't want to hear, but needed to hear, in her simple, direct way. Holding all the rest of us up somehow through everything. I was sure Cher would feel the same way.

Things went pretty fast after that. Mama got weaker and weaker. She just seemed to fade. We had built our house by then, set up high above the river a few miles outside of town, with huge front windows looking out over the scenery. We brought Mama home and set her up in a hospital bed in the downstairs study, so she could look out on the river and watch the birds. When she wasn't asleep, she had a procession of children marching in and out to talk to her, read her the Bible, put on puppet shows, and try and tempt her to eat. About the only thing she would eat were fudgesicles, or the new kind of ice cream bars made out of frozen fruit, so I kept the freezer stocked. We kept a nurse around the clock to keep an eye on her and monitor her pain meds. Mama stayed in our home all the way to the end, and that's how she wanted it. "No machines or fancy hook-ups for me," she said. She wanted to die with her family all around her, and if it couldn't be in her own little trailer, which she had refused to move out of even when I started making good money and wanted to buy her a new house, at least it could be in mine. When they wanted to move her to the hospital near the end, I put my foot down over that at least.

The Foxworthys came several times a week, and we generally shut the door on those visits. Mama seemed to relax with them like she did with no one else. Seemed like Mrs. Foxworthy was practically a mother to her, but I guess when Mama arrived in town as a pregnant teenager, scared and alone, that's pretty much what Mrs. Foxworthy was. I loved my Mama with every ounce of my being, but no matter how hard I tried to reign myself in, I always seemed to wear her out. Mrs. Foxworthy would walk in to Mama's room, shoo everyone away, and fuss with Mama's pillow and blankets. Mama loved it. She became compliant and content like a little child, and she could rest.

Sometimes, if she felt up to it, she and Jake would play checkers or cards, but Mama would tire after just one game. Then Jake would noiselessly pick up the pieces and settle in with his newspaper in the chair we'd put right next to the bed. Or he'd take a little doze himself, and we'd walk in and find them there, holding hands and fast asleep. Even though he was still healthy and going strong, Jake had passed his 80th birthday a few years back.

The night Mama went I busted up bawling. The doctor had

told us we were nearing the end, and I'd tried to prepare myself, but I just couldn't help it. I could tell it only made things worse for her, seeing me there crying. But I still couldn't imagine life without her there. All my life, when people said I was a half-breed and no good and would never amount to anything, she was there, telling me that was all nonsense, telling me I had good things in store for me, pulling me through. She wore out God's ears praying for me. Cher and the kids were going to miss her like crazy, and I was too. Things would never, ever be the same.

"Now Gus," she said, but she could barely talk, it was hurting her so bad. Her breath was coming in short, shallow gasps, and her eyes were shut tight against the pain. She waved her bony hand in the air, groping for mine. I grabbed it and held on tight. Then she seemed to rally a bit, because when she did speak, her voice came out strong and clear. "Now Gus, you listen to me. Stop your crying now, and let me go. I'm ready to go. I've done everything I meant to do. Jesus answered every prayer. I've seen you grow up safe and sound, you have your business and your family—look at you, you're a big success. I'm right proud of you, Gus. But you're a man now. You've got to be the strong one. You've got to be a like a rock, like a strong, deep cave. When things get rough, the weaker ones can come hide in you. Do you hear me now?"

"Yes, Mama," I said. I'd managed to stop crying, and I was straining to pick out every word. Her breathing started to come labored and fast again, but she managed to say, "I'll be seeing you all again now. And the children, too. We'll all be together again soon."

Then she cried out in pain, and started up in bed like a knife had gone right through her. Her hand gripped mine so hard my fingers started to turn white and tingle from loss of circulation. And for the first time I wanted Jesus to take her, to carry her away from all that pain. Then she laid back and said, "Oh . . . ," and her eyes were wide open. But she wasn't looking at us. She was looking off in the corner of the room. She let go of my hand and her body relaxed all over, and a little smile played on her lips and in her eyes. And then she was gone.

Cher walked over to my side of the bed, gave me a big hug, and whispered, "You're going to do just fine." Somehow, she knew just what to say. And then for some reason the picture came into my mind of one of those small, white butterflies, the common kind that you see everywhere in the summer. You watch them and watch them as they flit from flower to flower, trying to track them with your eyes, until they fly up and away toward the sky, and then they're just gone, they disappear right into the blue. Not the big flashy butterflies, the monarchs and the swallowtails that sit there preening on a leaf, waiting to get noticed. I'm not usually a poetic kind of guy, or one that sees pictures in my head, but it comforted me to think of her like that—flying right up into the sun, and vanishing into the light.

EPILOGUE

Practically the whole town came to Mama's funeral. Several people got up, and said some pretty amazing things. If Mama had been there she would have hated it. Adrian and Alex got up and recited some verses they had memorized, and then our four and five year olds, Ariel and Ashley, sang a little Bible song that had the whole room full of people grabbing for a tissue, dabbing at their eyes and blowing their noses, even the men.

Mama had been a quiet person. She'd kept mostly to herself. Outside of our little town, nobody knew her name. But she lived a good life. What she believed in, she lived, 100%. And the people who did get to know her more often than not were changed for the good.

As much as we all miss her, I can't help but believe she's right where she'd want to be. I hope she's in a big, fancy white house, with a garden full of flowers—the kind she wouldn't let me buy for her down here. Maybe if the Lord gave it to her direct, she would take it.

She was stubborn like that. But that's probably how she made it as a young woman.

In fact, I've come to believe that stubbornness and faith have a lot in common: Just flat out not giving up. Sometimes that's what it takes to get you through. I think that's a common man's definition of faith right there. You have your belief fixed in your head, and then you hold onto it like a life rope, and you just don't let go. Mama's belief was that everything God said about himself in the Bible was true, and no matter what happened, she held onto it. But here I might be getting over my head. That's the kind of topic Paul would take on, not me. God knows, he's got the education for it.

Paul came down for the funeral. He still isn't married, and maybe he was right, that afternoon so long ago when we were back in high school. Maybe he never will be. I hate to think that though, because he lives in his head and he thinks too much, and a PhD in Religion sure didn't help matters for him. A good wife might balance him out. You never know.

Acknowledgments

Thank you to all who have encouraged and supported me in writing this book. Especially:

My husband and children, who gave me time and space to write.

My parents, who have always been supportive of what I desired to do.

The Monday Mama's writer's group, especially Kayla Dawn Thomas —who, that afternoon at the pool with our girls, inspired me to get my story out of deep storage, and has made herself available with advice, encouragement, and helping me with all the technical stuff.

Bekah Croom, who submitted so many beautiful cover images that captured what I envisioned, it was very hard to choose.

And Jesus—without whom I would not be here to tell the tale.

About the Author

A. M. Nelson is a poet and writer who lives in Eastern Washington state. She is married with three children, and enjoys writing, reading, British mysteries, travel, gardening, and walking the dog. She posts poetry and thoughts on literature, faith, sexual abuse and recovery from PTSD, and other topics on her blog at http://www.angmnelson.com.

Made in the USA
San Bernardino, CA
08 November 2015